RULING WOLF

ETERNITY SHIFTERS - BOOK SEVEN

LOLA GABRIEL

SECRET WOODS BOOKS

Receive a FREE paranormal romance eBook by visiting our website and signing up for our mailing list:

SecretWoodsBooks.com

By signing up for our mailing list, you'll receive a FREE paranormal romance eBook. The newsletter will also provide information on upcoming books and special offers.

1

DARIA

I had been High Ruler Filip's second-in-command for almost a thousand years, so I was very used to his moods. He tended to hide his feelings under a layer of snark, so the fact that he was openly, intensely annoyed when I walked into his office took me aback.

"Good morning?" I stopped, watching him pace back and forth in front of the large glass wall on the far side of the room.

The wolf shifter in him came out when he was irritated; he moved like a predator, one moment from striking. It was hard to take my eyes off of him in moments like this, more out of awe than attraction these days. I still found him good looking, like many others did. His creamy brown skin, green eyes, and strong, masculine features were almost eerily perfect.

But the unrequited romantic feelings I had for him had faded. He and his mate, Mylee, were perfect together, and Mylee was too sweet not to like. I was happy for both of them. Having a mate was much more intense than just falling in love—you and your mate were bonded forever, able to feel what the other felt and willing to die for the other no matter what.

"Is it?" Filip stopped pacing and looked at me, his green eyes blazing. "I don't believe it is."

I resisted the urge to roll my eyes. His flair for the dramatic got a little tiring sometimes, but both me and Mylee were able to pull him out of it.

"What happened?" I asked, sitting down at my desk, adjacent to his.

Filip slid his embroidered red suit jacket off of his shoulders and hung it up before sitting down at his desk.

"Oskar happened," he said.

I sighed. Of course it was Oskar. No one got under his skin quite like the High Ruler of Northern Europe. I was almost impressed by how much their personalities clashed, like something deep in their brains made them oppose each other no matter what.

"What happened this time?"

A muscle in Filip's jaw twitched as he leaned back in his seat, crossing one ankle over his knee.

"We made a bet, and he got extremely lucky," Filip said, adjusting the photos of him, Mylee, and their daughter Audra that lined his desk instead of looking at me.

I raised an eyebrow at him. Didn't he know that I could read through his bullshit?

"So you lost."

"I just..." Filip waved his hand vaguely. "Didn't entirely win."

I snorted. "What was the bet about?"

"He bet me that Fyodor would clash with Aron at the High Ruler meeting," he said. "I didn't believe that they would argue, but they did."

I blinked, resting my forearms on my desk and studying him. I had access to all of the ins and outs of the High Rulers, their records and histories. Even I knew that the age discrepancy between Fyodor, who was approaching a thousand years old, and Aron, who was barely thirty, would cause an issue. Thirty years probably felt like they had happened over the span of a sneeze for Fyodor, and now someone that age, no matter how powerful, was technically equal to him?

Yeah, a recipe for disaster.

"So, you thought that the newest High Ruler wouldn't try to assert his dominance over one of the youngest High Rulers ever?" I asked.

Filip's nostrils flared as he blew out a breath, drumming his fingers on his desk. The tension in his forehead suggested that he was kicking himself on the inside.

"I'm not saying it was the best bet to make, but it was a bet that was made nonetheless." He lifted a shoulder in a casual shrug. "Is it wrong to believe the best in people? At least once? Aron has grown quite a lot."

This time, I raised an eyebrow. Filip had softened up quite a bit since he and Mylee had gotten together, but he was still himself—skeptical and sometimes flat out jaded. But he did have a small soft spot for Aron, even though he'd never admit it out loud. We'd both spent a lot of time with him as he acclimated to being High Ruler after being a nobody in rural upstate New York.

Prodding Filip about this stupid bet more wasn't going to get us anywhere, so I changed the subject.

"So what do you have to do?"

He sank back into his seat. "Keep in mind that I didn't pick this."

My stomach sank. "Oh, gods."

"Oskar would like you to come help with the falcon shifters in his region. There's been a lot of turnovers with conflicts and new leadership, so he'd like someone of your caliber, who's also a falcon shifter, to train them."

I blinked at Filip, waiting to see if that joke had a punchline. He was dead serious.

"What? Me? Why?" I asked, raising my voice slightly higher than I should have. Just because Filip and I were close friends didn't mean I could yell at a High Ruler. "You know how I feel about him."

If Filip had given me a choice between helping Oskar with his falcon shifters and eating glass, I would have chosen the latter. Oskar was just as irritating as he was handsome, to my frustration. Those blue eyes and lazy half-smile blinded people to the asshole underneath.

"I know that. He probably chose you to do this out of spite." Filip scoffed. "You'll have to leave at the end of the week."

"Wait, wait, wait." I held up my hand. "I can't leave. I help you with everything—what if you need me? Also, I don't know how I can help someone I hate. At least not genuinely."

"I know. But it's not forever, and I trust the others in my inner circle to help me while you're away," Filip said. "And if I need your insight, we have phones."

I sat back and crossed my arms over my chest. It was a little petulant to pout over this, but he'd blindsided me. I was old enough not to be a brat and sabotage Oskar, even though I hated him, but going there wasn't going to be a pleasant experience. Being around Oskar— no, just the thought of being around him—made my blood simmer.

"Think about it this way." Filip adjusted the sleeves of his shirt, revealing the golden sun tattoo on his inner wrist, signifying that he was High Ruler. "You go over there and do an incredible job, as you always do, and we'll both have something to hold over his head."

A wicked smile touched my lips. "That's very true. And it'll show him for what he said about falcon shifters."

It had been eight hundred years, but the fact that he found falcon shifters to be "weak and entirely superfluous" still irritated me. Who said that kind of thing to someone when they first met? I'd barely said hello to him when he looked me up and down with his ice blue eyes, sneered, and told me off.

Our numbers were much smaller than most other shifters, and we didn't have the physical strength of wolf shifters like him and Filip, but we were far from useless. Our skills were just different, not inferior. And apparently, he couldn't control us in his own region. He must have been desperate.

"Exactly," Filip said. "So, how do you feel about leaving Saturday morning for Iceland? That gives you a few days to train up someone just in case something big happens."

I fiddled with one of the piercings in my right ear. Did I have a choice in this? Not really. And Filip did have valid points about rubbing Oskar's failures in his face. But still, training a falcon shifter Ruler meant dealing with Oskar on a daily basis, which overshadowed everything else.

"I'm pre-annoyed by this," I said. "But yes, Saturday works."

"Pre-annoyed?" Filip snorted. "You seem extremely annoyed by it right this moment."

"Oh, I am." I jiggled my computer mouse to wake it up. "Trust me, it's only going to get worse from here."

2

OSKAR

I glanced up at the sky through the window in my office. It was frustratingly clear, a pale blue that extended across the plains, only broken up by the mountains still partially covered in snow. If the weather were in my favor, Daria's plane would have been delayed. And maybe even canceled.

Then again, her arrival was inevitable. And as much as it literally pained me to admit, I desperately needed her help.

Winning the bet against Filip felt good—it always did—but he probably sensed my desperation in asking this, as hard as I tried to play it off.

I wandered back toward my desk. My closest advisor, a fox shifter named Freya, was working away at her desk, adjacent to mine. She had somehow put her white-blonde hair up into a bun using just a pen to hold it in place.

"You've been wandering around the office like you're lost for the past half hour," she said, not even looking up from her computer screen. "There's no need to worry. I have everything under control for Daria's visit."

"I know. I trust you completely on that." I sat down at my desk again. "It's just..."

Freya finally looked up, lifting an eyebrow for me to continue.

"I don't think I gave Filip the full picture as to how dire our situation is, that's all," I said. "Daria is going to be furious when she hears how much work she has ahead of her."

"Won't she already be furious?" She pulled the pen out of her top knot, her hair falling to her shoulders. "She's Filip's closest advisor and friend. Usually, you hate the people who your friends hate."

True. Freya was a saint and didn't harbor negative feelings toward Daria, even before meeting her. Filip, on the other hand, was her least favorite of the High Rulers. He had humiliated me in front of my entire inner circle by beating me in a fight, back in my earliest days as High Ruler. It had taken me ages to regain their respect.

Granted, it was a different time, one where we fought more with our fists instead of using diplomacy, but still. I'd never forgiven him, especially since he kept trying to one-up me ever since. I was incapable of backing down from a bet or a challenge, which only spurred our conflict on over the centuries

"But she's good at what she does, so I assume she'll be professional and cordial." I sighed. "And she agreed to come. She could have said no."

"To her High Ruler? I doubt it." Freya noticed the sour look I had on my face because her features softened. "But if you say she's as good as you've heard, she'll do the right thing and help."

"I suppose so." She needed to help us, but I wasn't sure if anyone could. I pushed up the sleeves to my sweater. "Do you have the report on everything she needs to know ready?"

"I do." Freya stood, the sound of her high heels muted against the thick carpet, and handed me a booklet that was nearly an inch thick. I still preferred hard copies, but in this instance, I wished I'd just read the file on my computer. Its thickness was a stark reminder that our falcon shifters were flailing and spiraling out of control.

"Oh, wait, that's just the overview." Freya held up a finger. "Let me get the rest."

"Gods, are you kidding me?"

"Unfortunately, no." She pulled a large binder out from her desk drawer. "If it makes you feel better, it's filled with a lot of diagrams and maps."

I flipped through the booklet, which still had an alarming amount of text, separated by the issues at hand. Our smallest disaster—that I'd had to put half of the falcon shifter Alphas to death for conspiring to kill rabbit shifters en masse—took up a huge section. The rest of our problems were eighty times worse.

"Lovely," I said with a scoff.

"Well, there are a lot of problems going on right now. The fact that the old falcon shifter Ruler and his advisors had to be put to death for plotting to kill you is bad enough. Then, some falcon shifter Alphas had to be put to death for intentionally killing rabbit shifters for their territory. Throw in the fact that the new falcon shifter Ruler is practically an infant on top of that makes it even worse. It's a lot to deal with."

"Oh, come on, he's not an infant." I paused. "Twenty-two years old is an adult, basically."

"Sir, not to speak out of turn, but you mistakenly wrote the year on a document as 1954 the other week because time goes that quickly for you. Twenty-two years old is astonishingly young."

"Wait, did I?" I was probably distracted by the absolute disarray that the falcon shifters were in. I was on top of it otherwise, especially with Freya's help. "It's hard to tell with the way people dress these days."

"Fair point." Freya absently finger-combed her hair. "But seriously, the falcon shifters are in a very precarious position. My reports are very thorough and should give Daria everything she needs to get things in shape."

I rubbed my temple. "I hope so."

I skimmed through the reports that Freya and the rest of my inner circle had created, though Daria's looming arrival hung over my head and distracted me. Eventually, one of my security staff notified me that Daria had arrived. I let out a groan that I intended to be a sigh and went to my formal meeting room, my guards flanking me.

I wasn't sure what to expect—I hadn't seen Daria for centuries, and any correspondence we'd had was through professional means. Maybe she wouldn't dislike me as much as Freya suggested.

My guards opened the doors to the formal meeting room, revealing Daria sitting with a cup of tea near the window. She stood and bowed her head, as was custom in the presence of a High Ruler. With her eyes cast down, I took a moment to examine her. She was petite, even by human standards, but curvaceous in a way I appreciated even in her thick sweater and dark jeans—strong, but soft. Her long, wavy hair was dyed a vibrant red that played well off her fair skin and her deep blue sweater.

My attraction to her was bothersome, yet not intolerable. As soon as we talked more, the feeling would vanish into the background.

"Hello, Daria," I said, approaching her. "I hope your trip was pleasant. Welcome to my palace."

"Thank you." She lifted her eyes to mine for a moment, something I only allowed because she was of such high ranking, and the memories of meeting her last time came rushing into my head like a torrent. The fuzziness of me being absolutely trashed on shifter mead had prevented me from remembering before all of this, but her sharp brown eyes cleared up my thoughts.

I was an asshole to her the first and only time we met face to face, that much was clear. I'd said something about falcon shifters being weak, which was typical of me in that era. I didn't believe that now, but the fact that I had said it to her face was absurd. I held in a snort, but Daria wasn't amused. It had been so long. Was she still upset about it?

Regardless, I had changed, and I wanted to show her that I was capable of being professional. If I was begging my enemy for help, then I had to maintain my dignity and class doing it.

"I'd like to get started first thing in the morning, sir," she said, her posture rigid. "I have a lot of work to do."

"Of course." I smiled, hoping my pleasant expression would brighten hers, but she was just as closed off. "How can I make this visit more comfortable? I trust that my staff has treated you well so far."

She blinked as if she didn't understand me. "How can you make this visit more comfortable?"

"I know that Filip and I aren't on the best terms, but I asked you here for your expertise. You're a guest, and I treat my guests well."

She blinked again. Her almond-shaped eyes were captivating, a deep brown framed by dark lashes. I was so lost in them that I didn't notice how much time had passed in silence.

"Is there anything?" I asked again.

"No, thank you." She glanced at my guards. "I'd just like to rest."

"You don't want to join us for a meal? My chef can make you anything you'd like."

"I'm fine. You don't need to put on this polite act," she said. "We're not friends. We've disliked each other for a very long time."

I let out a low growl, and she immediately snapped back into line, looking down at her lap.

"We might be enemies," I said, even though she was the one who'd assumed that instead of trying to be cordial. "But that doesn't mean you can talk to me the way you might talk to Filip."

She murmured an apology, but I had no idea if it was sincere. I doubted it—she was probably only chastened because I had called her out.

"Meet me first thing tomorrow morning in my office for a briefing. Until then, my staff is at your disposal for whatever you need." I glanced at the guard near the door, then back at Daria. "My guards will take you to your room."

I got up and left without saying another word. If she was going to be difficult and not give me the benefit of the doubt whatsoever, I wasn't going to give it to her.

3

DARIA

I had been in Iceland for less than twenty-four hours, and I already wanted to strangle Oskar. Not that I ever could, since he was well over six feet tall and even more massive than I remembered, but a girl could dream.

And now I had to spend the whole day with him while he went through the mess the falcon shifters were in.

I bundled up to make the short walk from my quarters to the meeting room where I was going to be holed up with Oskar and his second-in-command, Freya. The views were stunning no matter where I was—one direction had plains and rolling hills, still hanging on to their summer, while the other had mountains in the distance, and the other had the ocean at the horizon. But the temperature left a lot to be desired. I was wearing more layers than three people combined, but I didn't care. It was only September, and it was fifty degrees, way too cold for my Floridian self.

Oskar had no control over the weather, of course, but I was mad at him for it anyway. Yes, I was being irrational, but something about him just flipped the wrong switch. Was it his ice blue eyes that always seemed to be laughing, even though I didn't find the joke funny? Or was it the way he'd tried to pretend that we'd never had an issue?

I wasn't expecting him to be hostile, but he was so overly polite that I didn't believe him for a second.

One of Oskar's many guards joined me without a word when I stepped into the cold. If I had to compliment anything about this experience, it would be his staff. All of them were impeccable in their service, which gave me a small amount of hope. Someone had to train them, so someone around here was competent.

I entered the main area of the palace, which had the Scandinavian design aesthetic with an opulent flare. The office where I was meeting with Oskar and Freya had the same design, and both of them fit right in with their pale blond hair, fair skin, and blue eyes. Oskar was dressed casually in a sweater with the sleeves rolled up and jeans, which looked frustratingly good on him, emphasizing his broad shoulders and muscled arms without seeming like the sweater was too small. Then again, he was wealthy beyond what most thought was possible, so it would be depressing if his style was still bad with all the help in the world.

He looked me up and down, likely in the same way I was looking at him. My face flushed despite that. If he said something about how bundled up I was, I was going to say something right back, but he didn't.

"Good morning," Freya said. She was wearing a sweater dress and heeled boots that made her even taller. I'd had a thousand years to get used to being short, but being short in her presence, when I wasn't in my home turf, felt different. She was me, but on Oskar's side —was she anticipating a rivalry? Or was that just me being on edge?

"Good morning." I glanced at the stacks and stacks of binders and bound reports on the table, along with a breakfast spread. "I'm guessing this is all the stuff we have to go through?"

"It is. Would you like some breakfast?" Freya asked, gesturing toward the lovely spread on the table. The food was very different than my regular breakfast taco, but the dark, seedy bread and various spreads looked good.

"Sure, thank you."

I sat down, and some of Oskar's attendants appeared to serve me. It was a little over the top, but I appreciated the attention nonetheless. Oskar sat directly across from me, but he was so long-legged that his legs brushed against mine. I pulled them back, shooting him a dirty look. Freya sat next to him, and the attendants came to serve them as well.

"Here's the overview booklet that I put together," Freya said, reaching across the table and handing me a bound book.

"This is the overview?" I looked at the spine, which was way thicker than any 'overview' had any right to be.

Freya cringed a little. "Yes. But diagrams and maps make up a solid portion of it."

Her definition of a solid portion was very different than mine because images only made up maybe ten percent of this whole document. Gods, what kind of mess were they in?

"To save time, we can give you a very short overview of everything." Freya opened a laptop and placed it so all three of us could see it. "Then we can decide where we'd like to focus our attention first."

"Sure, let's do that." I pulled out my notebook and pen, since taking notes on a laptop had never felt right to me.

Freya pulled up a presentation and hit start, glancing at Oskar, who was leaning back in his chair as if we were having a casual chat and not something that could destabilize his entire region. He sat up and cleared his throat.

"We'll go from most pressing to least pressing," he said, tugging a piece of bread in half and buttering it. "The most pressing is our falcon shifter Ruler. Unfortunately, the previous Ruler and his pack had plans to assassinate me, so I had to put them all to death. And that means a new Ruler and an entirely new team of advisors that need training."

I frowned. "That doesn't sound too difficult. Not that it'll be easy, but beings have had their entire Ruler leadership replaced before."

"The new Ruler is twenty-two years old and absolutely clueless.

The advisors were chosen seemingly at random, so we'll likely have to bring in new people who know what the hell they're talking about." Oskar popped his buttered bread into his mouth and took his sweet time chewing. "That's the problem. It's like handing over the power to a bunch of babies."

Freya raised an eyebrow at him for that, but he ignored her.

"Okay, that's definitely a problem." I wrote that down. "Do you have a file on the new Ruler? What's his name?"

"Gunnar Pedersen." Freya sifted through the stacks and stacks of binders until she found the right one. "It's over there next to you, sir."

Oskar grabbed it and passed it to me. Our fingers brushed together slightly longer than they had to. A tingle shot up my arm from the point of contact, and I frowned. Fine, I could acknowledge that Oskar was handsome, and I hadn't been with anyone in at least a year. That had to be the reason. He'd just touched my hand, for gods' sake.

"Thank you," I said, opening up the binder detailing Gunnar's background. Lovely, and it started right with his juvenile offenses for vandalism. "So, he's a criminal. I wonder why the Magic chose him."

"Small time stuff like vandalism. Hardly a huge deal. Who didn't get into trouble back when they were young?" Oskar asked. Once again, that blasé attitude of his stained the entire atmosphere of the room.

"It matters a lot. He's leading all of the falcon shifters in the region." I noticed a thin binder labeled *demographics,* which I assumed had the information on how many falcon shifters there were in the region. I flipped to the right page—the population was ridiculously small. At least that explained why the Magic had chosen him. It hadn't had a ton of options.

"Sure, but what about growth? He can grow," Oskar said.

"I never said he wasn't able to."

"You seem to imply that by harping on the one little thing he did."

"One little thing?" I flipped through the next few pages, scanning them. "He hasn't done much of anything. If he hadn't ended up as

Ruler, he probably would have bounced around from meaningless job to meaningless job."

Oskar sat back, crossing his arms over his chest. A glint of amusement shined in his eyes, and it took every ounce of my self-control not to punch a hole through the table.

"Is this funny to you?" I hissed.

"What makes you say that?"

I looked at Freya, whose mouth was tense. Was this what she put up with on a regular basis? How had she not flung herself into a crevice in a glacier or something?

Telling Oskar that was only going to provoke him, so I smoothed my hands over the pages in front of me and regained my composure.

"Okay, so Gunnar needs a lot of training," I said. "I'll put together materials for him to get up to speed, which will take me a few days, and then we can invite him in."

"Why not invite him sooner?" Oskar asked, a furrow in his brow.

"Because it's better to have everything thoughtfully prepared before bringing someone like him in." I glanced down at Gunnar's school records, which weren't anything to write home about. "It'll only be a few days. It's worth the wait."

"We'll bring him in and acclimate him to the lifestyle. It doesn't have to be so rigid, like school or something," Oskar said, shifting his legs so they brushed against mine again.

I pulled my legs back once more. Of course, he kept his in place, the asshole.

"You brought me here to advise and lead this process," I said, enunciating each word as if it would get through his thick head that way. "So why are you pushing back against my advice already?"

Oskar's eyes narrowed, and he sat up again, grabbing another slice of bread.

"Our secondary issue is that I also needed to put about half of the falcon shifter Alphas to death for conspiring to kill rabbit shifters over a land dispute, so we have a lot of new Alphas as well," he said as if I hadn't pushed back against him.

"So, essentially, the falcon shifters in your region are being led by a bunch of random leaders, and we need to fix that."

"More or less."

I flipped through the demographics binder to find information on the Alphas. He hadn't been exaggerating. His region had ten Alphas, and Oskar had executed five of them. And according to the careful cross referencing, each of them had a binder, too.

"This is a lot." I ran a hand through my hair, even though it messed up the style I'd carefully done this morning. "So, we can train Gunnar first, then move on to the Alphas. I'll need some aides to help put together the information for them. Freya, can you arrange that?"

"Of course."

"Is there anything else I'm here to help with?" I asked.

"No, not right now." Oskar pushed another stack of binders toward me, which toppled over due to its height. "By the way, here are the rest of the files on all the Alphas. They're much older than Gunnar, so you have your work cut out for you."

The binders were much thicker, so I peered inside one of them. Then another. And another. All of these Alphas were the bottom of the barrel, shifters who hadn't done much at all to show that they were good leaders.

When Filip told me that I was coming here, I assumed that I would have to train one or two shifters and be on my way. But apparently, I was tasked with putting the entire falcon shifter hierarchy back together.

My blood slowly rose to a simmer. "So, you've called me in to fix everything."

Oskar's eyes narrowed. "I wouldn't say that, necessarily."

"All of these documents say otherwise." I pointed to the stacks of information. "You expect one being to whip all of these leaders into shape? I'm good, but this is going to take months, even with aides to put together reports."

Oskar lifted his massive shoulders in a shrug so nonchalant that I wanted to scream. "So, it'll take months. That's what Filip gets for losing the bet. And you're not doing this alone."

I took a deep breath and let it out for as long as I could in the hopes that it would steady me. It didn't.

"Did you ask me to come here so I could fail?" I asked, leaning forward in my seat. "Because it seems like it. This project is enormous."

"No, I asked you here because you're a falcon shifter, and you're *almost* as good as Freya is." Oskar nodded in Freya's direction. "Why would I ask you to come here just to screw it all up? That doesn't make sense."

"Excuse me for not trusting you on your word." He'd always been sneaky. When he and Filip had made bets throughout the centuries, he always went for loopholes and anything else to make it easier to win. This time wasn't any different.

"You not trusting me isn't going to make this any better," he said, his eyes locked onto mine. The intensity of his gaze sent a shiver down my spine. "You're here to serve a purpose, then you'll leave. It's not any deeper than that."

I took a long sip of coffee, glaring at him over the edge of my mug. I had no reason to believe him whatsoever. Had he ever been honest? Straightforward? Nope. I was already tired of him, and I'd been here less than twenty-four hours.

If it weren't for Filip, I would have left already.

I glanced at Freya, who was sitting calmly, as if the tension in the room wasn't through the roof.

"So, what do you say?" Oskar asked. "Are you going to trust me or not? Are you going to help, or are you going to go running back to Filip with a failure on your record?"

I stood up, resting my hands on the table and leaning over it. It was long but narrow, so I got inches from his face without leaning over too hard. He didn't flinch.

"I'm not going to back down from this, period. Even if I have to work with you every single day, I'll get it done because I'm good at what I do," I hissed. "And then you'll owe both me and Filip. I doubt you'll be able to repay us for saving your ass."

His eyes flicked from mine down to my lips, then back before he scoffed. "Whatever you say."

Screw this. I gathered up the overview binder and stuffed it into my bag along with my notebook and pen. No one said anything as I stormed out.

4

OSKAR

"Well, that was eventful," Freya said once the sounds of Daria storming off faded.

I buttered more bread and put some smoked fish onto it, stuffing it into my mouth. Being pissed off and annoyed to the edge of my sanity made me hungry. I waved off the attendant who tried to put more food on my plate.

"I figured she'd be stubborn, but that was something else," I said once I swallowed. "Apparently, she thinks that she's here to take over for me."

"To be fair, you did ask her to come in to fix things. You can't be upset that she wants to, you know, do it." Freya pushed some of her oatmeal around in her bowl.

"I get that, but there's a difference between her helping and her stepping on my toes."

Freya gave me a look I knew well—she was tired of my bullshit.

"I think you're a little bit sensitive when it comes to her." Her pale blue eyes lit up in amusement. "Maybe you like her more than you're letting on."

"Like her?" I scoffed.

"Physically, at least." She finished her oats and pushed the bowl aside for an attendant to take away. "It was kind of awkward to witness."

"Sexual tension? Between me and Daria?" I asked, aghast. "Are you okay? What happened to my level-headed, astute second-in-command?"

Freya bit the inside of her cheek like she was trying not to laugh, which only made my blood boil. Nothing was happening between me and Daria. She was attractive, yes, but who cared? I was around beautiful females all the time, and it didn't faze me. Plus, personality went a long way in making a female attractive to me, so every bit of energy Daria put out turned me off.

Freya picked up on how serious I was moments later and calmed down.

"I'm sorry, sir. It was just...a lot." She folded her hands in her lap." Maybe we shouldn't have had all these binders out to overwhelm her. At least she got the overview. That should be enough to put together her initial reports."

"Her plans are a little bit too much. Putting together a report? A lesson plan?" I nearly laughed. "Shifters like that aren't going to be receptive to that whatsoever."

Freya shrugged. "I trust her judgment."

"I don't." Not entirely, at least. "Invite Gunnar over for dinner tomorrow, so he can see what life is like around here."

"Directly against her wishes?"

"Yes. I know what I'm doing." I stood up, and attendants rushed forward to clear my plates. "We'll have dinner and get a real sense of who Gunnar is."

I MANAGED to avoid Daria for the rest of the day and for the rest of the next day as well. I spotted her from time to time, walking with Freya or some of my inner circle, and went the other direction.

Was it cowardly, or was I just preserving my sanity? I was going with the latter. Daria had already put me on edge to the point where I wasn't getting much done. I had to take her in small doses. Plus, she was going to rip my head off when she realized who I had invited to dinner, something she was also going to attend.

"Sir?" One of my security staff appeared in my office doorway. "Your guest, Gunnar, has arrived."

"Excellent." I glanced at the clock on my desk. "A bit early, no? Is dinner nearly prepared?"

"Yes, it is. The appetizers are ready, and the table will be set shortly."

"Okay, bring him into the formal meeting room. I'll be there in a moment."

"Of course, sir."

I wrapped up my work and went into the small closet off the side of my office to pick something more formal than my usual sweater and jeans. I changed into a dress shirt and slacks, then headed to my formal meeting room, the same space where I'd met with Daria. My security opened the doors for me, revealing Gunnar across the room from me.

I had a picture of him, but knowing what he looked like didn't prepare me for what it felt like being in his presence. He was so incredibly young, appearing even younger than his actual age with the baby fat clinging to his cheeks and his gangly limbs. Dressing up to meet the High Ruler apparently hadn't crossed his mind, because he was wearing baggy jeans and a baggy sweater with some incomprehensible design on it. His hair was hot pink on one side and white-blond on the other, cut in some elaborate, gravity-defying style.

If I couldn't sense what being he was, a perk of being a High Ruler, I would have guessed he was human by his style alone. Then again, the younger generations were taking on more and more of human culture, to my chagrin. Keeping us separated was hard enough, but throwing in the internet made it harder to keep our existence a secret from humans.

"Hey, what's up?" Gunnar asked as if I were just anyone and not his High Ruler. Thankfully, he realized his mistake and got to his feet, averting his gaze. "Uh, sorry. Are we supposed to shake hands or something?"

Gods, we were screwed.

"It's fine. Beings typically bow their heads when greeting me, and you should typically avoid eye contact. But, those are things I suppose you will learn. Let's just move forward."

Gunnar nodded, looking back up at me. "Okay. It's nice to meet you."

"Likewise." I scanned his clothing. "For future reference, dinner with a High Ruler is always a more formal event."

"Oh." He looked down at himself as if he hadn't checked his reflection before he'd left the house. "Sorry."

I put on a smile, even though it likely looked like a grimace. "Will you follow me to the dining room? Appetizers are ready, and dinner will be served soon after."

"Sure."

Gunnar followed, and as we walked out of the room, my security flanked us.

"Is this a constant thing?" Gunnar asked, his eyes flicking to them.

"Yes, it is. They're highly trained and my first line of defense," I said.

"Even though you could probably kick everyone's..." He paused. "Even though you're stronger than everyone?"

"You know the reason why you're Ruler right now is because the previous one conspired to kill me, yes?" I turned the corner. "My security protects me from threats like that when my back is turned. Yes, I could defend myself—and you'll be trained to do so as well—but your security will be an extremely important part of your life."

Speaking of training, I spotted Daria down the hallway, talking to a dragon shifter in my inner circle. She was tiny compared to her, but something about the way she carried herself made her seem just as strong as anyone else. In preparation for dinner, she had changed into a black cocktail dress that hugged her lush curves and sky-high heels that made the elegant slope of her calf look dangerously appealing. I wanted to kiss my way up that calf and...

Gods, I needed to stop. It was Daria. No matter how good she looked in a dress, she was still a pain in my ass.

"That's Daria—she'll be training you," I said quietly, slipping into the next hallway so she didn't notice us.

"She will?" Gunnar craned his neck to look back at her, the interest in his eyes blatant, then jogged to catch up to me. "She's hot. Looking forward to training with her."

Fangs sprouted from my gums, and I growled at him before I realized what I was doing, making all the color drain out of his face. The rush of anger inside my chest took me aback, and I stopped walking.

"She's come here from the States to whip you into shape, not to be your eye candy. You'll treat her with respect," I said, getting into Gunnar's space. He backed up into the wall. "Understood?"

He nodded, averting his eyes. "Understood."

"Good." I straightened the sleeves of my shirt, my fangs retracted, and I kept walking.

Gunnar was silent the rest of the walk, as was I. I had just been complaining about Daria. Why had I reacted so strongly to Gunnar's interest in her?

I didn't know, but either way, I wasn't looking forward to seeing Daria at dinner. Gunnar was going to be an unwelcome surprise.

5

DARIA

I had a near photographic memory of the laws surrounding High Rulers: what the punishments were for attacking one, conspiring to kill one, and so on. I had no intention of being executed, so I couldn't appease any of the murderous urges coming up within me when I laid eyes on Oskar and the shifter I recognized as Gunnar next to him at the dining table.

He had brought Gunnar here for dinner *directly* against my wishes? How dare he? Did my input not matter at all?

And somehow, Gunnar looked even more child-like now that I saw him in person. Everything about him contrasted what I envisioned as a Ruler. I loved dying my hair and had regular appointments with my hairdresser fae to maintain the charm that kept my deep red hair looking fresh. But I kept the color somewhat neutral because I was in a professional setting, working with professional people. And I wasn't going to even touch whatever was going on with his sweater.

Despite the storm of emotions raging through me, I put on a cordial smile and entered the room, bowing my head toward Gunnar.

"You must be Ruler Gunnar," I said. "I'm Daria, and I'll be in charge of training you for your new role. It's wonderful to meet you."

"Nice to meet you, too," Gunnar said, his Adam's apple bobbing as he swallowed.

The dining room was formal but small, the rectangular table taking up most of the room. Oskar was at the head of the table, and Gunnar was adjacent to him, so I sat across from Gunnar. Looking at Oskar pissed me off, especially since he looked like he was born to wear the suit he was in, so I turned my attention to Gunnar instead. But the longer I looked at Gunnar, the more the pit in my stomach grew. I expected raw material to work with, but he was *very* raw.

An attendant appeared by my side.

"Would you like something to drink?" she asked.

"A cocktail would be nice for now. Anything is fine as long as it has some fae liquor in it," I said.

The attendant disappeared, leaving the room in uncomfortable silence again. The appetizer spread was the only thing in the room that appealed to me, so I took a few of the canapés and put them on my plate.

The table was set, but not in a way it would be for a truly formal dinner. The chef was probably going to serve us three courses, max. I put my napkin into my lap and picked up my fork.

"So, how was the trip here, Gunnar?" I asked.

"Fine. I live in Iceland, so I didn't have to go that far." Gunnar messed with his forks.

"Great."

The silence lingered so long that I finally stole a glance at Oskar, whose face was set in a neutral expression. Gunnar picked up his glass of shifter mead and guzzled it like we were at a party and not a semi-formal dinner. Was Oskar seeing what I saw?

The attendant returned with my drink moments later, placing it down.

"I propose a toast," Oskar said, lifting his untouched glass of wine. "To Gunnar and his future success as the falcon shifter Ruler."

Gunnar snorted. He actually snorted, as if he thought it was a joke. Gods, if he didn't believe in himself, how was I going to teach him anything?

Oskar and I locked eyes for a moment, but we tapped our glasses together anyway. Gunnar finished off the rest of his mead. I didn't blame him. If my cocktail weren't so strong, I would have chugged it too, just to take the edge off this awkwardness.

I straightened up and took a measured breath. I had dealt with far more awkward and tense situations as Filip's second-in-command. Handling a completely unprepared Ruler wasn't going to break me.

"So, how has your experience as Ruler been so far?" I asked, since Oskar wasn't saying anything. He had invited Gunnar, and he wasn't going to try to engage in conversation? Typical.

"Kinda crazy, if I'm being honest." He ran his hand through his hair. "I had to move out of my apartment into the headquarters, and now all these people are waiting on me hand and foot, even for stuff like getting water. And I don't get to go out with my friends or anything. I have to sit around and pick a council or attend to business."

He said this without an ounce of self-awareness. Did he not realize that he was whining like someone even younger than he was? I waited for him to say more, to redeem himself, but he just stuffed a canapé into his mouth.

"It'll become more of a routine once you're trained," Oskar said. "Daria is putting together a plan for you."

He looked at me expectantly, as if I was supposed to spout off the entire plan I'd hardly put a dent in. I nearly choked on my cocktail. He *had* to be kidding me. So much for telling me that he didn't want me to fail. He was underestimating me—I'd spent most of last night at my desk, trying to put together this plan on a faster timeline.

"It'll be a mix of everything you need to know—self-defense, protocol, laws, procedures," I said. "I'll be starting with the self-defense aspect, since you're here sooner than I anticipated."

"Like how to fight?" Gunnar looked even paler than normal. "Like fist fight?"

"Yes, fighting in your human form and your falcon form, like I mentioned earlier," Oskar said. "Is that an issue?"

"No, I just assumed that it was a thing that came with the magic. Like I'd just *know*." Gunnar shrugged.

"No. It's hard work, and you're going to be doing a lot of it. You might be physically stronger now that you're Ruler, but you need to hone those skills," I said.

"It's basically like school," Gunnar said. "With learning all of the stuff."

"It's just training. You won't get grades," I said. "Your true test will be how you lead."

Gunnar went even paler, somehow. An attendant appeared by his side with another drink, which he took with a mumbled thank you. He downed it so quickly that I feared he'd be wasted by the end of the meal.

Wait staff came with our first course, a warm soup that smelled delicious. I watched Gunnar as he took the first spoonful of his soup, just to get a feel for his table manners. He held his spoon like he'd never used one before and slurped his soup.

"This is amazing," Gunnar said, eating faster.

"It won't run away from you," Oskar said.

If anyone else had said it, I would have found a trace of humor in it, but my stomach was sinking faster and faster.

"Do you have any questions before we begin?" I asked.

Gunnar was too busy having a love affair with his soup, which he got a second bowl of, to make small talk. And something in my gut told me that he wasn't going to ask any unless prompted.

"So, I'll be trained in everything I need to know. When do I get breaks?"

"Breaks?" I said, hoping I misheard him.

"Yeah, like, how long is every day? What about weekends?"

"Being a Ruler doesn't come with many breaks. Anything could happen in the falcon shifter world at any time, and you're the first shifter they'll go to. You'll be able to take vacations eventually, but not any time soon," I said. "As for your training, I'm not sure. Expect at least twelve-hour days."

Gunnar did little to hide the horror on his face. What did he expect? That the leader had a bunch of time off?

I took a deep breath. I believed in the Magic—it was the invisible force that created magical beings and chose every High Ruler and Ruler. And before today, I believed it chose the best being for the job.

But Gunnar turned my view upside down. A thousand years of existence, and he'd blown that belief to bits in half an hour. I almost admired him for being so egregiously awful without any of the self-awareness that I assumed came with adulthood.

I finished my soup. Maybe I was being too harsh on him. Clearly, his life had been entirely carefree before. His records said that he had graduated from high school and coasted off of his inheritance ever since, hanging out with friends and making questionable art. This abrupt change to a world of fairly strict decorum, non-stop responsibilities, and pressure would have been hard on anyone.

"That blows," Gunnar finally said, clearing his throat.

Oskar locked eyes with me, a hint of worry in them for the first time since I'd arrived. Lovely. I had my work cut out for me.

6

———————

OSKAR

I hated being proven wrong. Inviting Gunnar here early before Daria was ready was a complete mistake. Dinner was a disaster on every level—Gunnar's table manners, his attitude, and his lack of intelligence. All of it.

As High Ruler, I had a stronger sense of the Magic than others. But gods, had it made the wrong decision this time. Were falcon shifter numbers so low that he was the best option? Maybe I needed to create incentives for falcon shifters to try to have children. Magical beings rarely ever had children, and if they did, they probably had one or two, tops. It was an uphill battle, but clearly, one that needed to be fought.

I woke up early, as always, and went to my office to handle a few issues since most of my day was going to be spent with Daria and Gunnar. My stomach was in so many knots that I didn't have anything but coffee for breakfast.

Daria had emailed me late last night with the schedule for today, and it was probably going to be more than twelve hours. Most of the day was going to be spent going through self-defense, then the basics of dining decorum. She had probably moved the latter up after seeing how Gunnar ate like a feral animal during dinner.

When the time came for the start of Gunnar's session, I dragged my feet to the open space in the palace that I used for training. Daria was standing on the far side of it, dressed in leggings and a snug long-sleeved shirt that hugged her curves in a distracting way. I forced my eyes elsewhere. Her puffy coat was folded over the back of one of the chairs. The weather wasn't nearly cold enough for that.

"Is our training session going to be outside?" I asked her.

She raised an eyebrow at me, then went back to whatever she was doing on her tablet. "What?"

"The coat." I pointed to it.

"It's not my fault that everywhere else is too cold," she shot back.

I snorted despite myself. "Let me guess—he's late?"

"Of course he is." She slipped her tablet back into its case and set it aside. "Also, we have to start with this because you brought him here before I was ready. It would be better if we started with the soft skills."

"He needs help with absolutely everything," I said.

"I know that." Daria huffed, checking the time on her phone. "But at least with this, he has some raw strength and better coordination than a regular falcon shifter."

She had a point.

My ears picked up on Gunnar talking to one of the guards as he walked over. The kid was a mess in every way, but at least he was friendly most of the time.

He came into the room, and once again, I was surprised at how ill-suited he was to the occasion. I needed to lower my expectations. He was in sweats and a t-shirt, but both of them were made for fashion, not function.

"Hey, sorry I'm late," Gunnar said. His eyes went to Daria, particularly her body. I growled just loud enough for him to hear, but not so much that Daria would, and he looked away.

"You're here, so that's all that matters at the moment." Daria approached him, her expression all business. "First, we need to get a sense of your abilities. Have you done any martial arts training?"

"Oh. I've never fought anyone in my life. Unless you count

hunting in my falcon form as fighting," Gunnar said with a nervous chuckle. "I'm very much about peace."

Another point in his favor, though hopefully, he wasn't a coward.

"Well, your enemies don't share the same sentiment." Daria walked back toward the middle of the room. "Come here. We'll go over the absolute basics."

I sat down on the sidelines and watched. Gunnar wasn't as uncoordinated as he looked. Then again, nearly all shifters had some physical ability, especially birds.

But he didn't know a damn thing about fighting. The only thing he was going to beat up was himself. Daria flung him around like a rag doll once they graduated from punches and kicks to grappling. At least he got up to his feet relatively quickly?

I was grasping at straws.

"Let's take a break," Daria said.

Gunnar rushed over and flopped into the seat next to me. Unlike Daria, he was drenched in sweat. He guzzled water that someone had left nearby.

"Maybe your training plan is a little bit too..." I tried to think of a way to phrase it in the least offensive way possible. "Advanced."

"I've put together training plans for all of Filip's security, and they're the best at what they do," Daria shot back.

"Filip's security members were hired because they already had some fighting abilities. Gunnar just learned how to throw a punch forty-five minutes ago," I said. "And he's barely able to do that. Fix your methods."

"This shit is hard," Gunnar mumbled, his tone so whiny that my irritation grew tenfold in an instant.

Daria crossed her arms over her chest. "How do you think I should do my job, then? If you're so great, why don't you spar with me? I'll treat you the way I've treated past trainees."

I grinned. "Oh, you know that I can't turn down a challenge."

I got up. Standing next to her heightened the different between us. She had to be kidding me—she came up to my chest. Even with all the training in the world, I was always going to be stronger and faster than her. But we were just going to spar, so I'd only use a fraction of my strength. I hardly needed any to put her in her place.

We squared off, facing each other in the middle of the room. I anticipated her first strike with ease, dodging it. Same with the next. I hadn't sparred against such a small opponent before, which threw me off, but never enough to give her the advantage.

She was holding her own without holding back. I absorbed her punches, but she was much stronger than I thought she'd be.

"You don't need to hold back *that* much," Daria said, huffing.

"You're underestimating my strength."

She scoffed. "You're underestimating mine."

"Fine."

I attacked her again, throwing a fast punch near her middle that she barely dodged. After going back and forth for a while, I saw an opening to grapple her to the ground and took it, slamming into her. She grunted with the impact of us hitting the floor, rolling us onto our sides. I'd knocked the breath out of her, but she recovered faster than I thought she would.

Taking her to the ground was a big mistake. She was so small that she could move underneath me with ease, slipping past my defenses like they were almost nothing. I should have known she'd have the upper hand down here since brute strength wasn't as important.

We tussled for a few moments before she managed to get above me. She straddled me, trying to pin my arms, which was great for her...not so much for me. Her shirt had ridden up, exposing a strip of skin, and sweat made her face flushed. Her positioning easily transitioned in my head to something else—to her riding me until both of us came so hard we saw stars.

She took that millisecond of distraction from me and pinned my arms and one of my legs.

Shit.

I got out of her grip, getting back to my feet. She did the same, her chest heaving. Even though I'd been chastising myself moments ago for being distracted by her gorgeous body, I got distracted again. Her sweat had made her clothes cling to her curves even more, and her top was still pushed up around her waist.

"Let's shift," I said as casually as I could. Her being in her falcon form was the only way to keep my head on straight, apparently.

"Fine. Similar rules? Light contact?" she asked.

"Of course."

I shifted, as did she. Being in my wolf form felt like returning home in some ways—the changes in my perception, being lower to the ground, being able to run even faster and farther. I wished we were outside so I could run in the fresh, clean air, but I'd do that on my own later.

Daria was in the air above me, her powerful wings flapping. Her bird form was fierce looking. She had the same razor-sharp gaze that she did as a human, and her wings had a reddish hue to them. It had been decades since I'd sparred a bird shifter, but I looked forward to the experience.

"Ready?" I asked her telepathically. As a High Ruler, I was able to communicate with any shifter in this state, while other shifters could only communicate with beings of their own kind.

"Ready."

The ceilings of the room were high, so she flew up toward them, circling me. I followed her, crouched down and ready to leap into the air when I had the right opening.

But she found one first, dive-bombing me like a rocket. I darted out of the way, nipping one of her wings. She landed moments later, fluttering the wing out like she was hurt.

"Was I too harsh?" I asked.

"No."

Then again, I doubted she'd tell me if I had been. We went back and forth, her swooping down at me and me dodging. She was relentless, hardly letting up. If she were going against any other wolf shifter, she would have beaten them readily. She was more than holding her own against me.

"I think we've proven a point, no?" Daria landed on the rafters above

after several more minutes of sparring. *"Can I get back to training him, please?"*

"Fine."

I shifted into my human form again, keeping my back turned as I pulled my clothes back on.

I retreated to the seats, glancing at Daria, who seemed almost entirely unfazed by the fact that we'd more or less beat the shit out of each other. The way she rolled her shoulders was the only indication that she felt the effects of the fight.

She went back to training Gunnar, who had more energy now that he'd had some rest. They shifted into their falcon forms and sparred that way, too.

Watching her work with him now gave me a new appreciation for her skills. She was pushing him but holding way, way back from the best of her abilities. Getting any more basic with him was probably impossible for her.

She had impressed me, not that I'd ever tell her to her face. Ever. Maybe she was the one being who could turn Gunnar around.

7

—————

DARIA

The next few days stretched me to my limit. If I wasn't training Gunnar, I was working on my curriculum for him, adjusting it to address his bigger faults, or preparing for all of the Alphas to visit. And if I wasn't doing any of those, I was trying to keep my head on straight with Oskar hovering around all the time.

The High Ruler was so damn infuriating. He wasn't with Gunnar and me all day anymore, but when he was, he had (fairly useless) opinions. And when I told him to maybe let me do the job he had brought me here to do, he just gave those opinions through those ice blue eyes of his. His gazes were potent.

I swallowed, slipping into my heeled boots. Everything about him was potent—his presence, his attitude, and admittedly, his attractiveness. Something about the vaguely smug, carefree attitude mixed with his high cheekbones, blue eyes, and thick blond hair just wiggled its way under my skin.

I threw on my coat and gathered my bag, trying to ignore the faint thrumming between my thighs at the memory of our grappling match. Straddling an opponent wasn't a huge deal to me—a fighter was able to pin down whoever they were fighting that way.

But straddling him? With his broad-shouldered body beneath me and my core dangerously close to parts of me I needed to keep locked down while I was here?

I hated myself for it. This was Oskar. Having any feelings toward him besides vague animosity was a recipe for disaster.

I made my way to the main part of the palace, where Oskar's staff had set up a large conference room for the meeting with the Alphas. Someone else had printed the booklets I'd put together, which hadn't taken me long to make. I'd brought Alphas up to speed in the past, so I only had to adjust it to fit this situation. This very unusual situation. I had never heard of five Alphas being appointed all at once.

"Good morning," one of Oskar's staff, a female wolf shifter whose name escaped me, said when I entered.

"Good morning. Everything looks perfect." I looked around the table. "Could you remind me of your name, please?"

"My pleasure." She rushed over to help me with my coat. "My name is Lucy."

"Lucy." I smiled at her. "You've been an amazing help so far."

Her cheeks colored. "I'm glad to be of help. High Ruler Oskar should be here in a few moments."

"Thank you." I sat down near the head of the table, pulling out my notebook and tablet.

I had given Gunnar the morning off under the guise of giving him a break, which had thrilled him to no end. In reality, I wanted to feel out how the Alphas were before introducing Gunnar to the mix. He was still a raw lump of clay, and from the profiles I had, all of these Alphas were older than him. Underestimating how much age came into play with these power dynamics had led to the bet that had landed me here.

I went over the agenda for the morning, then for the rest of the day. Oskar came in moments later, trailed by his guards. Today he was wearing a sea green sweater that made his eyes look a similar color, and dark jeans.

"Good morning," he said, breezing by me and sitting adjacent to me. "Ready to meet all of the Alphas?"

"More than ready." I nodded toward the documents in front of him. "As you can see."

He crossed one ankle over his knee and leaned back in his chair, as if he were about to read a novel and not a fairly important document. I bit the inside of my cheek. Saying something about it was the best way to get him to talk back at me.

"Good." He absently flipped through it, not reading a word.

I let the silence stretch between us before I lost my will to stay quiet. "You don't want to go over the agenda?"

"We'll go over it together, won't we?" He lifted one of his massive shoulders in a shrug. "Why do it now?"

"Filip always goes over my agendas and notes, so he won't come across as unaware," I said.

Oskar snorted, a smile spreading across his face. It gave him dimples, which were infuriatingly endearing, even on him. "You know I'm not Filip."

"Of course not. I don't feel like screaming at Filip every other second," I said with more venom than I should have. We had traded barbs back and forth the entire time, but I was mindful of the line between disagreeing and disrespecting a High Ruler. As much as I hated him, I respected his title.

"I don't believe that for a second." He burst out into a real laugh, which echoed across the room. "He's easily the most punchable male I've ever met. He wears capes sometimes, for gods' sake. And that's not even touching what comes out of his mouth."

"I'm extremely familiar with how you two interact, so no need to rehash the past." I glanced out the window. My vision was extremely powerful, so I noticed the little details of a human town way off in the horizon. Outside of Reykjavik, the country was so sparsely populated that I hadn't seen any actual humans within miles of here.

A knock on the door brought my attention back into the room.

"Come in," Oskar said.

"Sir, the Alphas are here. May I send them in?" his guard asked.

"Yes, go ahead."

The guard opened the door all the way, and all five of the Alphas entered—three males and two females. None of them had said a word, but their annoyed energy spoke for them. Was it because of the meeting? Or each other?

Alphas ruled over their individual packs, so they rarely had to work together on day-to-day tasks. But in order to keep things from escalating up to the Ruler or High Ruler, they often collaborated on bigger issues. Hopefully their annoyance wasn't interpersonal. They'd been here for less than twenty minutes. How bad could it have been?

Each of them bowed their heads in deference to Oskar, then took seats around the table.

"Good morning," I said, standing up. "I'm glad all of you are here. I'm Daria, and I'm here to bring you up to speed on being Alphas and what issues are currently going on in the region."

"Where are you from?" one of the female Alphas named Ulla asked, cutting me off. She crossed her arms over her chest.

"I'm from the southeastern region of the United States. High Ruler Oskar brought me here since I'm a falcon shifter, and I'm the second-in-command to High Ruler Filip," I said.

She studied me for a moment, as if she were looking for cracks in my armor, but she didn't say anything more.

"Since all of you haven't met before, why don't we start with introductions?" I sat down. "Then we'll go over the agenda and start with the first item on it."

"I'm Ulla," she said without prompting. "Alpha of the Ice Falcon pack."

The two male Alphas on either side of her tried to go next, so I had to mediate that as if they were children. Overall, we had Ulla, Klaus, Artem, Annelli, and Pasha.

"Thank you," I said, going back to the agenda. "So let's—"

"Excuse me, but why isn't High Ruler Oskar running this meeting?" Klaus asked. He had a reddish-brown mustache that made him look even more severe than his strong brow did.

"Because he's extremely busy. He's here to meet all of you, and I'm here to train all of you for the next few weeks. I've done it countless times." I sat up straighter. With males like Klaus, who were all muscle, I had to assert myself more. I wasn't sure why some still equated size with power.

Klaus didn't like that answer, but I wasn't in the business of being liked. I glanced to Oskar for backup, but he didn't speak.

"We'll start with the basics of what being an Alpha means and do a brief overview of all the topics I'll be training you on for the upcoming weeks," I said.

"I already know what being an Alpha means," Artem said. He tugged at his knit cap, which covered his bald head "Why do we need to go over it? All of us are more than old enough to understand."

"Maybe some of us want to hear what she has to say." Annelli leaned forward and glared at Artem. Oddly, she looked just like him, with her own knit cap over her buzzed hair "To be better Alphas."

Artem pressed his mouth into a line. "If you need to study how to be good, you won't be good."

I blinked. What kind of moronic logic was that? Instead of saying what was on my mind, I said, "Being an Alpha has a lot of nuances to it that even those closest to them don't see. That's my goal here—to get all of you to be the best Alphas you can be and to work with Ruler Gunnar to ensure peace and happiness for the falcon shifters in your region."

"Where is Ruler Gunnar?" Pasha asked, as if I were in trouble for withholding him.

"He'll meet with you this afternoon," I said.

"Why not now?" Pasha shot back.

"Because he's busy." I once again glanced at Oskar, who looked pretty damn amused at everyone acting like petulant children who weren't getting snacks at daycare. The asshole. Even if I took the lead, he could have at least pretended to care. "Now, can we begin?"

I started going down the agenda, and the Alphas didn't get much better. If they weren't taking verbal swipes at me, they were taking verbal swipes at each other.

And what did Oskar do? Nothing. Even if I addressed him directly in the hopes of getting some kind of support, he only said a few words.

By the time our lunch break arrived, I was fuming.

"Meet me back here in one hour," I said before storming out.

"Daria, come here," Oskar called after me. With his long-legged stride, he was able to catch up to me with ease.

I didn't stop until I rounded the corner.

"Why?" I asked, whipping around to face him.

He glanced both ways down the hall—we were alone.

"Because this entire situation is crumbling," he said, his voice so sharp that the hair on the back of my neck stood up. "They're not respecting you whatsoever. Get them under control, and clean up this mess."

I nearly screamed. How did he not see the problem here? Or did he see it, and he didn't want to take any accountability for it? I wanted to tear out all of my hair, then his. Instead, I kept walking down the hallway toward the door that led outside.

"Daria." He moved astonishingly fast, backing me into a small nook in the hallway that only had a painting in it. "Don't walk away from me again. Explain yourself."

"You're pissing me off because you don't see that you're half the problem!" I hissed. "Gunnar barely wants to be Ruler, but all of these Alphas sure seem to want to be in charge. And none of them trust me, no thanks to you. I'm from another region, and they don't know me whatsoever. Your trust in me is extremely important!"

"What am I supposed to do? Tell them to like you?" Oskar scoffed, looking down the hall again. "I could, but I can't reach into their heads and change their minds. All of them are stubborn."

"You can at least back me up!" Being this close to him made his clean scent fog up my senses. "Say something. Support me. Tell them to back off."

"You know you would have bitten my damn head off if I intervened for you." He got even more in my space, his neck flushed in his anger.

"No, I wouldn't have. Don't assume that I'll act a certain way." I swallowed. We were way too close to each other. Maybe he wanted to be hidden by the nook we were in.

"My assumptions are correct most of the time. The point is that you're screwing up, and you need to fix it."

"You're absolutely exhausting. We're going in circles here since you can't wrap your head around being even slightly wrong." I glared up at him, my breath coming in shallow pants for some reason. He smelled too good, and his closeness made him even more imposing in a way that made my knees weak. "I shouldn't have expected you to lift a single finger or give a—"

His lips came crashing down on mine, his big hand cupping the back of my neck. My already weakened knees buckled, but I supported myself by digging my fingers into the soft fabric of his sweater. The kiss was almost bruising, all anger and frustration tied up in lust.

His hands skimmed down to my waist, then my ass. And that woke me up.

I shoved him away from me, catching him off guard. Both of us stared at each other, our chests heaving. If my lips looked as freshly kissed as his did, everyone was going to know what had happened.

For once, he was at a loss for words. I shoved past him, breaking into a jog toward the door leading outside. He didn't call after me.

I burst outside, the cool air stinging my burning hot face. How had I let lust get in the way like that? He had just let me screw up in front of a group of shifters who needed to see me as an authority. I had even more reasons to hate him than before, a fact that had to stay in the forefront of my thoughts.

8

OSKAR

The awkwardness between Daria and I after I kissed her was new and strange to navigate. The usual irritation that radiated from her whenever we interacted had turned into hesitancy and excessive formality.

I wasn't sure if I was any better. Being around her only brought up inconvenient memories of how perfectly she had fit against me, all those soft curves, and how much angry passion her kiss had had. And those thoughts made my blood simmer. This was Daria. She didn't like me, and I didn't like her. Supposedly.

What had made me snap like that? The intensity of our argument? The way her brown eyes blazed? Her sweet and spicy scent up close? I half expected her to kick me in the balls, but she had kissed me back with just as much intensity.

And it felt *right*. It shouldn't have. But both of us clicked.

My guards were opening the door to my office too slowly, so I shoved past them, opening it myself. I wanted to get this discussion of the progress Gunnar and the Alphas were making over with. It was a shitshow, that much was clear. And as much as the memories of our kiss had taken over my head, what Daria said before had still landed.

Yes, I'd sat back and let them try to steamroll her. If she was so hellbent on not taking my direction, I'd let her suffer the consequences on her own. But the disrespect the Alphas had showed her made me angry all over again. I easily imagined punching their heads clear off their bodies, and holding back that urge was more difficult than it should have been. I shouldn't have cared, given the position I was actively putting her in. I didn't want to think much about that urge, either, since it only made my rage burn brighter.

Freya and Daria were working at the small table I kept in the corner with a great view of the landscape outside. Freya looked up, but Daria didn't.

"Good morning, sir," Freya said.

"Good morning." I sat down at the table, my knees brushing Daria's. She pulled her legs back like the touch burned her. Today, she was wearing a black sweater that exposed one creamy, smooth shoulder. The elegant line of her neck, fully bare because her hair was in a ponytail, tempted me in ways I hadn't anticipated before I sat down.

"Sir?" Freya said, as if she were repeating herself. Was she repeating herself? I was too distracted by Daria.

"What?" I asked.

"Lucy asked if you needed anything, sir."

I looked toward one of my attendants, Lucy, standing near the door. "Coffee."

She bowed her head. "Would anyone else like anything?"

"I'd love coffee as well," Daria said.

"I'm fine with my tea." Freya tapped her mug.

Lucy disappeared to get the coffee, leaving the room quiet and awkward again. At least awkward to Daria and me. Freya's full concentration was on her laptop screen before she looked up again.

"Daria and I were talking about the next steps in Gunnar's training," Freya said. "We both feel that we need to press him more. More physical training and classroom training. Longer days."

"You think that's best?" I asked Daria. "He's not exactly doing the best at the moment with the days we have scheduled."

"Here's my proposed change of plans." Daria picked up some

papers next to her, tapped them on the table to even them out, and handed them to me.

How had she already put this together? She worked fast. I thumbed through the pages, even though her plans were always solid, at least from a technical standpoint. Getting Gunnar to go along with it was another story.

"This looks fine," I said, handing her the papers again. Our fingers brushed when she took them back, sending tingles up my arm.

"You're sure?" Daria raised an eyebrow.

"Yes, I'm sure." I raised one back at her. "Why?"

"You accepted it readily." Daria put the papers down next to her laptop, straightening the edges. "You don't have any opinions?"

She laced the word "opinions" with a touch of annoyance. I swallowed, guilt making the back of my neck heat.

"Not at the moment, no." I shifted in my seat, extending my legs and touching Daria's again. She glared at me, but I kept my legs in place. She could move if she didn't like it. We stared at each other for a beat before she pulled her legs back.

The silence felt heavy for reasons that weren't clear to me yet. The subtle twitch of Freya's eyebrows told me that she had picked up on it, but Lucy returned with our coffees before getting the chance to break it. The drink was already prepared the way I liked it, with a heavy pour of cream.

"Thank you, Lucy," Daria said with a smile when the attendant put down her coffee.

"My pleasure." Lucy smiled in return, as if they were friends.

Were they friends? I'd put Daria in the "unpleasant and unfriendly" box in my head for so long that the idea of her befriending someone in a lower status than her didn't fully compute. I took a long drink of my coffee to hide my slight frown. I didn't want to think of Daria differently, but evidence of her not being who I thought she was beat me over the head every other second.

"So, we should discuss Gunnar's progress in more detail," Freya said, shutting her laptop and cupping her mug of tea in her hands. Her expression was grave.

Daria sighed, stirring sugar into her coffee. "I don't want to sound pessimistic, but his progress is much slower than I'd hoped, hence the change in my plans. I'm trying to throw everything at him in the hopes that some method will stick, but it's not working."

"Your plans look flawless to me," Freya said, resting her hand on a copy of the binder of plans Daria had given us both.

"I know they are, not to sound cocky. But he's just..." Daria looked at a point way off in the distance, her eyes weary. "Difficult. He doesn't naturally have the competitiveness and drive that most Rulers are born with, and his subordinates will see him as weak. He doesn't want to do this, so he's not trying. And I can't train that out of him."

"The Magic chose him. He can't ignore that," Freya said.

"The Magic has chosen plenty of people who weren't ready." I drummed my fingers on the table.

"I don't think it's a matter of him not being ready," Daria said, more annoyance in her tone. "It's a matter of him not wanting to be ready, ever."

"So, you want someone to make him want this role?" I scoffed before I could stop myself. "This isn't the kind of thing that people grow to want. If anything, the more he learns, the more he'll pull away."

The moment the words were out of my mouth, I regretted it, even if it was true. Daria's face flushed, more out of irritation than embarrassment.

"It doesn't matter. What does matter is that he has to be Ruler now, and clearly, the falcon shifters here have reached the bottom of the barrel," she said. "Whoever will come after him will undoubtedly be worse but in a different way. He needs your guidance, if you decide to put more effort in."

I bit the inside of my cheek to stop myself from saying something else that was out of line. If she hadn't thrown on the last part of that sentence, I would have readily agreed. But the stubborn part of me, the part that was still holding onto the grudge that we'd had against each other for ages, didn't want to give into her so easily.

"I'll consider it," I said.

"Fine." She didn't hide her skepticism at all. Her phone rang on the table next to her, and she tilted the screen to see who it was. "Excuse me. It's a call from Filip's headquarters, and I need to take it."

She took her phone into the hallway, answering it on the way out. Once the guards posted outside closed the doors behind her, Freya looked at me in a way I was all too familiar with. She was rightfully about to tear me a new asshole in the quiet, gentle way of hers.

"Sir, I understand Daria's frustrations," she said. "I think we need to put the past behind us and actively work together to get Gunnar up to speed. His lack of will is a much bigger problem than his lack of everything else."

"You don't need to convince me," I replied. "I agree."

Freya blinked. "You do?"

"Is that so surprising?"

"You just said you'd 'consider' guiding Gunnar after Daria expressed real concerns about his desire to even do this job." She snorted. "Apologies for my shock."

I raked my hand through my hair and slumped in my seat. "It's just hard to let go of everything between us. It's like my brain has carved out the path of least resistance in our interactions with each other, and that path is always against her."

"I'm sure you two can figure it out." Freya glanced toward the door.

"We have to." I finished my coffee. "If I don't, I'm just creating problems for the future."

"Very good point. And she'll be gone by then, so it'll all be on our shoulders."

I looked out the window onto the gray day outside. Being High Ruler meant that I was faced with huge problems regularly, but the burden of my problem with Daria was heavier. My attraction to her was undeniable, and we'd ripped the lid off that can with our kiss.

But I wasn't doing myself any favors by constantly resisting her. I had to meet her in the middle, for everyone's sake.

9

DARIA

Working with Oskar's inner circle was much more of a pleasure than I ever thought it would be. All of them were smart, hardworking, and proactive in dealing with problems. But even the Alphas tested their patience. I'd tasked them with helping me train them, since I had to give Gunnar so much attention, and all of them reported back to me looking like they'd been through battle.

Dimitri, a bear shifter from Oskar's inner circle, was the latest victim. He trudged into the office space I'd been given, his enormous shoulders slumped.

"Bad news, I'm guessing?" I asked.

"Let me tell you about it." He sat down, the chair creaking under his weight. Most bear shifters were big in their human forms, but he was easily one of the biggest males I'd ever seen. He gave me a rundown of how their work was going. It was a mess, of course, but I listened, taking in everything he said with a neutral expression.

After giving him a little advice on how to proceed, he left. I pulled some chocolate out from my desk drawer and dug in. I always had some on hand for stressful days, but I'd never gone through so much of it before. Usually it eased my stress—today, it didn't.

The weight in my stomach that never went away these days pulled me down as I got ready to meet with Gunnar. Nothing had improved after my conversation with Oskar and Freya about Gunnar's lack of will. Granted, it had only been two days, but time was of the essence. All of the regular tasks that Alphas and Rulers handled were stacking up higher and higher, and Oskar's inner circle could only handle so much while helping me with the Alphas.

Oskar's reluctance to even talk to Gunnar made my blood boil. I shouldn't have been surprised, though. Despite the argument we had before we'd kissed, I hadn't seen him throw himself into the process like I'd hoped. I needed to lower my expectations with him as well. Him saying he'd "consider" talking to Gunnar about being Ruler was him telling me "no."

I was in this on my own. Even though I was here as the result of a bet, I never did anything halfway. I was going to do my best and leave. Oskar and his inner circle had to deal with the consequences.

I said hello to his staff and inner circle on my walk to meet Gunnar. How were all of them so cooperative when Oskar was such an asshole? The discrepancy bothered me. If Oskar was as smug and lazy as I found him, wouldn't the people he chose to be around him reflect that? Every last one of them was great.

I pushed that thought aside as I came into the conference room, expecting it to be empty since Gunnar was always late. But he was there. I almost didn't recognize him. Sometime between our last lesson and today, he'd gotten a relatively normal haircut, and it was all his natural pale blond color.

It did wonders for how he looked. Instead of appearing like some random shifter who'd stumbled into being Ruler, he looked like someone that people could see as a leader.

"Oh! You changed your hair," I said.

"Yeah, I did." He ran his fingers through it and chuckled, not meeting my eye. "It's still weird."

"It looks great." I sat down adjacent to him, putting my stuff down. "What made you decide to change?"

His cheeks flushed, and he shrugged. "Dunno. Got tired of it."

So suddenly? Something about that didn't sit right with me, but I didn't care. He looked more professional, and the change made me more optimistic than I'd been since I had started training him. And on top of that, he was wearing a more normal sweater—black with strange tassels here and there, but it wasn't neon or filled with holes —and jeans.

"Let's get started," I said, opening up my laptop. "Were you able to study the treaties we started talking about yesterday?"

"Yeah." He tapped his tablet to wake it up and opened up a notes app. He had taken actual notes? "I got up to the falcon shifter and warlock treaty of 1056."

"That's great." I scanned my notes for today's session. I hadn't anticipated him actually studying ahead, so we could skip most of today's lesson plan. "Tell me what you gathered."

Gunnar scrolled down in his notes, biting his bottom lip in concentration. He hadn't lied about anything so far, so I assumed he'd actually studied up until that treaty. Going through all of the historical treaties that falcon shifters had made over the entire history of magical existence was tedious, but I had to make sure that he grasped the most important ones that were the basis of our laws today.

"Okay, so the treaty basically made it so warlocks and falcon shifters weren't at war anymore, and that the warlocks had to..." He scrolled more. "They had to assist the falcon shifters with rebuilding their region. And also, the treaty made it so we have a warlock ambassador to the falcon shifters and vice versa to keep the peace."

"That's exactly right." I tried to keep the awe out of my voice but failed. Gunnar hadn't analyzed a single historical document on his own and gotten the most important points correct before. "Can you tell me more?"

Gunnar swallowed, his Adam's apple bobbing, and launched into a more detailed explanation. He got all of the major players right— more or less—and was able to tell me about the past ambassadors and their contributions to falcon shifters in the region.

From there, we went down the rest of my lesson plan. The bored look in his eye that I'd become accustomed to was gone, and he actively took notes instead of insisting that he just "had it all" in his head. He even asked an insightful question here and there. Since getting him to engage wasn't like pulling teeth, we zoomed through the lesson plan with plenty of time to spare.

It was a miracle. And I was pretty damn suspicious. Yesterday, he'd been the same checked-out shifter as before, and now he was almost a model student.

"Great work today," I said, closing my books. "You've clearly been working really hard."

Gunnar blushed even more. "Yeah. And thanks."

"What made you change, if you don't mind me asking?"

"High Ruler Oskar came and talked to me yesterday." Gunnar messed with his hair again, as if he still wasn't used to the short length. "Talked to me about it."

"He did?"

"Yeah. I guess I've been having a hard time accepting the fact that I'm Ruler," he said. "I mean, I'm not the smartest or the best at anything, to be honest. Like, I can name four different guys my age who would have been better at it. But he made me see it as an ongoing thing that I can come to like if I put in the effort. No need to resist it if the Magic saw something in me."

I nodded, trying to absorb the fact that Oskar had actually done what I had suggested. And done a good enough job at it that Gunnar was taking this seriously. My heart softened toward him just a fraction, as much as I hated to admit it. Gunnar clearly admired him now.

"That's great," I said. "So, you're excited?"

"I mean, I'd rather not, but I'm going to make the best of it." He smirked. "Oh, and he told me to get my hair cut."

"I figured." I stood up, gathering the rest of my things. "It looks nice. Makes you look more like a Ruler."

"Seriously?" He grinned, which made him look painfully boyish. "Nice."

I snorted and patted him on the shoulder. "Get some rest, okay? We have a lot more studying to do."

"I will."

I left, heading back to my quarters, my mind hazy with questions. Was Oskar doing this to cover his own ass in the future, as he should have from the start? Or was he giving the kid advice because he cared?

I glanced over my shoulder at the building as I walked away from it. I had the feeling that this wasn't just Oskar covering his ass. Maybe he wasn't as bad as I thought. The very idea of that made me feel itchy in my skin.

10

OSKAR

The weather cooled down more and more over the next few days, which I usually didn't mind. As a wolf shifter, I was resistant to the cold even in my human form. But it meant that Daria was piling on more and more layers, covering up all of those curves I'd become addicted to. Now I only saw her body when I dropped in on Gunnar's self-defense training, which I had less and less time to do.

Because I saw Gunnar's training less, the leaps in his abilities between sessions were massive. When I pulled him aside to chat about his role as Ruler, I never thought my words would actually get through to him. But he'd actually taken them to heart and was doing ridiculously well. Better than I ever thought possible, if I was being honest. I'd been more candid with him than I had planned to be, but it had paid off.

My guards opened the door to my office for me, where Daria was waiting at the table. She still had a hat on and was once again bundled up as if it were freezing. It was around four degrees Celsius, so hardly enough to warrant that.

"Do you want someone to light a fire?" I asked.

"Hm?" Daria looked up, surprised that I'd appeared. When she was focused, she was completely into whatever she was doing. Her dedication to her work was admirable. "Oh, sure. It's getting cold out there."

She tugged off her hat, her long red hair sticking up. She smoothed it, her hair getting caught on one of her intricate rings.

"Shit," she murmured, trying to untangle it.

"Here, I've got it," I said, gently freeing her strand of hair before she asked me to. It was silky soft. That kiss exploded into my memory again, how it had felt to dig my fingers into her hair. It was just long enough for me to hold onto as she took me—

"Can I have my ring back, please?" Daria asked.

"Sure." I dropped it into her hand, my face burning. I sat down to hide the rapidly developing situation in my jeans. "Is it really that cold here for you? It's only four degrees."

"I don't know what that translates to in Fahrenheit, but it sounds way too cold." She checked her phone. "It's forty Fahrenheit. Back home it's...eighty. Perfect."

"Daria, you're a thousand years old, and you're still operating in Fahrenheit?" I shook my head and smiled. "Why? It makes absolutely no sense."

She snorted and looked away, as if she were embarrassed to have let it out. "Some habits die hard. It's stuck with me for some reason."

The air between us was comfortable, as if we joked around all the time. I rubbed the back of my neck, the usual tension returning the moment we both noticed it was gone.

"Anyway, Gunnar," I said, running my hands along my thighs. "How is he doing?"

"He's doing very well," Daria said. "You saw him yesterday during his fight training. He's gotten much better at using his strength and speed. And he's really been applying himself on the soft skills, though he's still behind in the decorum aspect. But in terms of his dedication, it's night and day."

"Excellent. You've been doing a great job," I said.

She blinked several times, her eyebrows going up. "Was that a compliment?"

"It was."

"So why are you telling me this now? What changed?"

"The obvious." I resisted the urge to fidget with something and made myself maintain normal eye contact. "He's doing better with your training."

She clicked the end of her pen, looking at a point past my head. The furrow in her brow made me stay silent, not wanting to disrupt whatever thoughts she was stringing together.

"He said you spoke to him about being Ruler a few days ago. That you made him see things differently."

Her eyes were softer than I'd ever seen them, and it tugged at some part of me that I didn't know existed.

"I spoke to him, yes." I broke eye contact, a knot in my throat.

"After you spoke to him, his attitude changed." She twisted the ring that had gotten stuck in her hair around her finger. It had an oval-shaped, rough-cut red stone in it. "What you said really made a difference."

"What do you mean?"

"I mean that it resonated with him," Daria said. That gentleness in her eyes wasn't a fluke—it was still there, wearing me down, too. "What did you say to him?"

I blew out a breath, sitting back in my seat. In most circumstances, I would have kept my mouth shut tight. But resisting her was getting exhausting. Something had shifted in her, breaking down the wall that had been up for centuries, or at least breaking down part of it.

"I told him that I related to him," I said, my voice low. "That I'd felt like the Magic had chosen wrong at certain points in my life. I've been to dark places in my time as High Ruler."

The room was still, as if she wanted me to continue.

"About a thousand years ago—a little before we met for the first time—I made a big mistake. I was too cocky and ignored what a lot of my inner circle was telling me about a conflict between two large wolf shifter packs. I thought that because I was a wolf shifter too, that I knew better than anyone else. But I didn't, and the two packs fought. So many lives were lost, and it was so easy to avoid."

I swallowed. Even though I'd processed this incident, it still hurt to talk about it. Having to walk onto the field where they'd fought, all of that red blood on the white snow, was never going to leave my thoughts.

"At first, I felt the way Gunnar did—that the Magic had clearly chosen wrong. I drank a lot and blew off responsibilities. But feeling that way wasn't going to bring anyone back, and it sure as hell wasn't helping me rule anyone else. So, I made an effort to do better. My past wasn't going to determine my future."

Daria's hand twitched like she was going to reach for something, maybe my hand, but she stopped herself.

"I never knew that," she said, her voice barely above a whisper.

"I never advertised it." The corner of my mouth quirked up. "It's also probably why I was an asshole back then."

Daria swallowed. "Ah."

"Not that it makes it better, but I was an ass to everyone." The air between us was getting too serious, so I smiled. "It's one of the few times where I completely understood why Filip hated me."

Finally, she smiled, too.

"Thank you for telling me. That all makes sense," she said.

What did that mean? I didn't want to ask since the idea of hearing the answer terrified me. Whatever it was, it had softened her all the way.

The space between us seemed to close. Was it because of me, or because of her? One of us had shifted so our knees were touching. That overwhelming urge I'd felt in the hallway, the one to kiss her, rushed up inside me like a flash flood. I started to lean forward to close the gap between our lips, but Daria sat back, clearing her throat.

"Um, I need to go," she said, gathering her things. "Was that report enough?"

"Yeah, it was." Either way, she was already on her feet.

"See you later."

She rushed out as if she were on fire. So much had happened all at once, and I was reeling from it. Where did we stand now?

11

DARIA

I shut the door to my quarters, my chest heaving as if I'd been running for miles. The cold air stung my lungs, so I breathed into my hands for a second to warm myself up, my back glued to the closed door.

What was wrong with me? Oskar told me a nice little story, and suddenly, I was putty in his hands? I had almost kissed him again. What had I been thinking?

I pulled off my coat and my sweater, leaving on my thin long-sleeved shirt. The fabric stuck to my skin, and I pulled it away from my stomach. Next, I yanked off my hat while toeing off my shoes. Putting my hair back in order reminded me of how delicately he'd extracted my ring from it without my asking. That simple touch was like a bolt of lightning going through me.

I threw myself onto my bed face down. Dramatic, yes, but I reserved the right to be this way when part of my worldview had been flipped upside down. Oskar had always been the smug, cocky asshole to me. The guy who had been a dick to me for no apparent reason. Filip's enemy, the one who always tried to one-up him because of some old rivalry he refused to let go of.

He wasn't the male I'd seen—the one with a great, devoted staff who respected him. The one who had opened up to some lost kid and made him turn around completely. The one who had nearly kissed me again.

For a moment, I indulged myself. What would his kiss have felt like this time, now that we weren't mad at each other? Soft and tender? Or would it spark the lust that had been simmering inside of me for weeks now?

I rolled over onto my back, staring at the wooden beams across the ceiling and absently rubbing my sternum. I didn't like considering two separate sides of one person at war with each other in my head.

Throwing lust into it made it even more complicated, but I could chalk that up to my lack of sex. Oskar was the kind of handsome that went beyond the surface in an unquantifiable way. His features weren't particularly unique, but the way he expressed himself made his face captivating.

But what was going on beyond his looks? I trusted Filip—I was closer to him than I was to anyone else in the world—but was their rivalry based on a lie? How could Filip hate someone with many of the positive qualities that he also had as a High Ruler? Was it an instance of them being too similar to one another deep down?

I pulled my phone from my pocket and sat up, scooting with my back toward the headboard. Thinking about Filip and everyone back home made me homesick. The only time I'd talked to Filip had been brief and about a business matter, but that had been a while ago. We'd texted and emailed in between, but we hadn't had a chance to catch up at length with both of our schedules being so hectic.

I still had access to his calendar on my phone and saw that he had a block of free time right now. My thumb hovered over his contact in my phone. Did I want to ask about his rivalry with Oskar?

I started a video call with him and immediately decided against bringing up his relationship with Oskar. I was too mixed up myself to talk about it in any coherent way.

"Daria?" Filip answered with his phone facing a perfectly blue sky. Then, he adjusted the angle so I could see his face. He was on the beach with Mylee and Audra, who were off in the background. Seeing them made my heart ache, too.

"Hi. Just calling to see how things are there," I said.

"They're good. I should be the one asking you what's going on there. We haven't had the chance to speak about how it is in enemy territory." Filip sat down in a beach chair. He had a private strip along the water, which he'd outfitted with every luxury possible. "How is it?"

"It's fine," I said. "Drastically better than it was."

"Yeah?"

"Yeah. It was a complete mess when I started. The new Ruler is ridiculously young and didn't have an ounce of desire to actually *be* the new Ruler. But he's turned it around, and he's doing well."

"At least there's that. What made him change? Finally realized that there's nothing he can do about what the Magic chose?"

If I told Filip the truth, he wouldn't believe me.

"Something like that," I said. "But the new Ruler is the least of my worries now. The Alphas are a complete disaster so far. Power games and fighting all over the place. They barely trust me, much less anyone else in Oskar's inner circle who I've tasked to help me."

"Alphas? Craving power? I wouldn't have guessed." Filip snorted, glancing off to the side where Mylee and Audra were. "I'm sure that you can wrangle them. You've wrangled everyone else you've been tasked with."

"Thanks." I sighed. "It doesn't feel like it."

"Oskar isn't giving you trouble, is he?" The warning tone in his voice made the hair on the back of my neck stand on end. How did he manage to do that through the phone?

"No, no." At least not in the way he thought. "He's been fine."

Filip raised an eyebrow. "Oskar? Fine?"

I got up and wandered toward the window to ease the sudden antsy feeling in my legs. My room faced a massive courtyard, which had other visitors' quarters around it, too. It wasn't busy at this time of day aside from a few of Oskar's inner circle and various guests wandering through.

"Yeah, fine," I said. Lying to Filip made my stomach churn, but the alternative was worse. "I don't see much of him. His inner circle has been helpful."

"Good." The edgy tone in Filip's voice disappeared. "If he gives you any trouble, just tell me, and I'll have it handled."

"I've got it, but thank you." I was about to tell him more about Iceland, which I hadn't gotten to see much of, but a commotion broke out at the edge of the courtyard. I frowned.

"What's going on?" Filip asked.

The noise was from two of the falcon shifter Alphas, Klaus and Artem, in each other's faces and shouting.

"Oh, gods. The Alphas." I waited, hoping they would cool off, but Klaus shoved Artem. "Shit. I have to go. I think I need to break up this fight."

Filip shook his head. "Good luck. Bye."

I was halfway out the door by the time he hung up. My room was only on the second floor, so I ran downstairs, bursting out into the courtyard. Some of the other Alphas and members of Oskar's inner circle were trying to break it up, but Klaus and Artem were still incensed.

"Don't pretend. You know exactly what you were doing," Klaus said, stepping into Artem's space despite someone trying to hold him back.

"You're just paranoid!" Artem wasn't trying to back off, even though Klaus was the aggressor. "Do I need to tell you in three other languages for you to get it?"

"Hey!" I shouted, pushing my way through the crowd. "What's going on here?"

For a moment, I feared they'd brush me off like they were ignoring Oskar's inner circle, but thankfully, they stopped.

"He started throwing out accusations about me flirting with his mate!" Artem said with a scoff. "I wouldn't do that even if she were single."

"So now you're insulting my mate, you—"

"Relax, both of you." I stepped in between them. "You can't fight like this, especially outside. You're Alphas. You're supposed to be an example, not two lowlifes who fist-fight over something like a mate. Klaus is bound to his mate, and everyone can see it. Mates don't cheat on each other. Put this bullshit behind you."

Klaus and Artem stared at each other for a moment, the anger still simmering between them. Finally, Klaus stepped back, scoffing, and stormed off to his room.

The crowd that had gathered dissipated, and my shoulders relaxed. Artem didn't thank me—he left as well.

Would the issues ever end? If the Alphas got set off on something as ridiculous as that, I didn't have much hope for their futures.

12

OSKAR

Despite the new leadership changes among the falcon shifters, I still had to deal with the ongoing issues in my region. And today, I had a meeting with the rabbit shifter Ruler, Anja, who had been trying to get a meeting with me for over a week.

Guilt crept its way up my spine as I went to the small meeting room where Anja was waiting. Rabbit shifters were rarely a problem. Since they weren't predators, they didn't fall victim to the same infighting or power struggles as wolves or dragons or falcons.

But they were still vulnerable after the former falcon shifter Alphas had tried to kill several high-ranking rabbit shifters over a land dispute. I needed to pay more attention to them, even if I doubted they'd retaliate.

"Anja, hello," I said as I entered the room.

She stood, bowing her head before sitting down again. I hadn't seen her since I had sentenced past falcon shifter Alphas to death, so she looked more or less the same: petite with extremely long pale brown hair tied up in an intricate bun. She dressed modestly in a shapeless gray sweater and darker gray pants.

"Apologies for how long it took for us to put this meeting together. It's been busy lately," I said, sitting down.

"The falcon shifters?" She sat and folded her hands in her lap. Her face didn't betray any emotions, but I assumed she had feelings about it.

"Yes. We're training the new Alphas and bringing them up to speed." I hadn't heard anything good from the training aside from the fact that it was happening, so I left it at that.

"Oh." She pursed her lips together.

"The new falcon shifter Ruler is coming up to speed as well. It'll be a new era," I said. "A peaceful one."

"I hope so, because I asked for this meeting because of falcon shifters. Again." Finally, Anja showed a hint of irritation.

"Tell me what's going on."

"We're trying to rebuild after the deaths." She swallowed. "We're still having issues with certain falcon shifters coming into rabbit territories to hunt. They claim they're going for non-shifter rabbits, but it's too close in my opinion. I lost a family member to one of these hunts. Trying to talk to the falcon shifters isn't getting us anywhere."

"This is unacceptable, Anja." That guilt that I felt earlier reared its head. "Thank you for bringing it to my attention. Where is this happening? I don't want any more bloodshed."

"It's in western Norway," she said, showing me a map of exactly where on her phone. "One of the areas without an Alpha at the moment."

Great, so Ulla was the Alpha in charge of that area. She wasn't the worst out of them, but she was far from the best.

"Okay, the new Alpha and Ruler will be made aware of the situation. It will be handled, or they will have to deal with me," I said. "For now, I'll send extra security to avoid any further conflicts."

Anja bit her bottom lip. "Who's the new Alpha? May I meet with them?"

"Not yet, no," I said, my words coming out in a rush. Ulla was far from ready for a diplomatic talk. "But we'll have a big meeting with everyone together after their training."

"Okay," Anja said. Her tone said it wasn't, but she didn't fight me on it. I didn't like any of my Rulers being unhappy, but I was glad that rabbit shifters were passive most of the time. I'd fought enough shifters lately.

"Is there anything else you'd like to discuss?" I asked.

She brought up a few additional matters before leaving. I watched her leave, a weight in my stomach. Clashes between different beings, especially ones with such different powers like falcons and rabbits, brought up unpleasant memories.

I went back to my office right away and asked Freya to start helping with the rabbit shifter issue before going to sit in on another one of Gunnar's protocol lessons. Despite the changes he'd made since I had talked to him, protocol and anything that involved remembering social decorum was a weak spot.

The guards held the door open for me as I entered. Daria looked moments from throwing in the towel, her long waves mussed as if she'd been digging her hands through it in frustration. Gunnar was slumped in his seat, wearing a huge hoodie and baggy jeans. He was always pale, but he looked even paler, almost like he was hungover. Was he? He had talked about how he used to party all the time, but even in this stressful situation, he hadn't had a lot to drink.

Both of them greeted me despite their moods, and I greeted them back, sitting down.

"I just wanted to see how things were going," I said.

"We're going over the typical events a Ruler has to put on every year," Daria said, annoyance written all over her face. "And the protocol for each one."

Gunnar didn't respond verbally—he just lifted a shoulder as if he didn't think that was true.

"Which one are you on?" I asked him.

Daria opened her mouth to respond for him, but I held up a hand to stop her.

"Um..." Gunnar scrolled around on his tablet. "Summer solstice?"

"We're on winter solstice," Daria said. "Please, Gunnar. This isn't that hard. Whoever you choose for your council will help you out with this, but it's important that you know what you're going to be putting on and why."

"I know." Gunnar ran his hand through his hair, sliding even lower in his seat.

"Are you sure you're feeling okay?" Daria asked.

"Yeah, I'm just tired," he snapped. I gave him a warning glance, and he straightened up. "Sorry."

"Let's get back to it. To the winter solstice celebration," Daria said.

She quizzed him on the important historical context for the celebration, and he got everything wrong. Some of it was stuff he should have just known as a magical being, like the date of the solstice every year. I locked eyes with Daria over the table. Her jaw was so tight that I was surprised her mouth was able to open to speak.

"Let's take a break," Daria finally said, looking to one of the attendants standing near the door. "Could we get some coffee in here, please? Maybe some tea to give us a boost?"

"Of course."

The attendant disappeared, and Gunnar left after her, looking down at his phone. Once he was gone, Daria rested her elbows on the table and pressed her face into her hands. I reached out and gently touched her elbow, startling her into pulling away. So she wasn't into being comforted with touch. Good to know. Still, a tinge of disappointment settled over me.

Our almost-kiss had joined our actual kiss and our sparring match in my fantasy bank. What if she hadn't left? What if I'd actually kissed her then?

"He's not doing well?" I asked instead of focusing on us. Gunnar was the bigger issue here.

"No." Daria sat up. "He's regressed almost entirely. It's like he's even worse than we were in our very first lessons."

"He seems hungover."

"He does, but he won't admit it. I didn't smell any alcohol on him, though."

"I didn't, either."

"I don't know." Daria shuffled the papers and books she had in front of her around. Her frustration made me want to step in and fix things for her, just to get rid of that furrow in her brow.

"I can talk to him again," I said. "See if he's reverted back to his old way of thinking?"

"No, it's fine. I have it under control." Daria's voice was clipped.

"Fine." I waited for her to look at me again, to acknowledge that our relationship had changed, but it hadn't. "Are you okay?"

"I'm fine. I can handle him." She looked past my head as the attendant returned with a tray of coffee and tea.

"I can see how he'd wear on you. One step forward, two steps back," I said, keeping my voice as gentle as possible.

"I can handle him," she repeated.

I thanked the attendant after she poured me coffee the way I liked it, wishing Gunnar would get back already. Daria wasn't interested in talking with me. Was it just because of Gunnar? He hadn't negatively impacted her mood like this before. Was it me? Or us? In my head, an "us" was forming.

Gunnar returned, bleary eyed, and Daria started his lesson again. My eyes lingered on her, though not for how attractive I found her, which was the usual reason.

The last time we were in a room alone together, we had nearly kissed. Something had shifted then. But it had shifted back already, and I wasn't sure why. She was so close to letting go with me entirely. The feelings were there, not that it meant she wanted anything serious. What was stopping her from seeing how good releasing that pressure valve could feel?

13

DARIA

I never got used to how intense Oskar's eyes were. The rest of the lesson yesterday, he watched me carefully, picking up on every shift in my mood as if he were tuned into my brain. Just the memory made me shiver. He got to me like no one else had, wiggling his way underneath my defenses, which kept falling.

He wanted me. My body wanted him. But just letting it happen was such a dangerous idea. My hatred for him was gone, a fact I had become comfortable with. But whatever these other feelings were pushed me to places I had never been before. I'd had a few serious relationships, but mostly just flings to pass the time.

Having Oskar's full attention after centuries of that was too much. And all of our history on top of that...

I took my mug of tea and walked toward the window of my little office, my heeled boots clicking on the floor. I didn't want to think of him, at least not now.

After staring out at the stunning view for longer than I should have, I went back to my desk to get more work done. Gunnar's sudden regression yesterday had rocked my confidence in getting him up to speed. Was Oskar's talk with him just a fluke? Or was he honestly hungover and unwilling to tell me?

I checked in with the members of the inner circle who were handling the falcon Alphas, answered some messages from back home, and prepared for my next session with Gunnar. We'd skipped the sparring today to catch up on the soft skills, so we had a lot to cover.

In the late morning, I gathered my things and went to our lesson room. He'd shown up early or on time for our lessons when he was engaged with the program, but yesterday, he'd been late. The minutes dragged by as I waited for him to show up. Ten minutes late was his usual, but twenty minutes had gone by. Then thirty.

I texted him, since he'd never pick up a phone call. No answer.

I sighed, getting up and pulling on my coat again. His quarters weren't far, but I hadn't adapted to the weather enough to walk in just my sweater. I went up to his room, where two guards were standing post outside.

"Hi. Is Ruler Gunnar inside?" I asked them.

"Yes, he is. He's still resting," one guard said.

I frowned. "Has he come out at all this morning?"

"No, ma'am."

I checked my watch. It was noon, so he might have been asleep. But my gut told me not to make assumptions.

"Let me in, please," I said.

The guard reached for the door handle, but he stopped. "We were told not to..."

"Let me in," I repeated, glaring up at him.

The guard did as I asked and opened the doors. A lamp was on in the corner, providing the only light in the room. His curtains were drawn, only a sliver of light peeping through.

"Gunnar?" I called, walking farther into the room.

A lump was on his bed, presumably him. A tuft of his blond hair stuck out from the covers, as if he'd burrowed underneath them.

"Gunnar." I put my hand on his shoulder and rocked him. "Gunnar, you're late for your lesson. Wake up."

He didn't stir. I sighed and shook him harder. Still nothing. That gut feeling blew up into a knot of anxiety in my chest, and I pulled the blankets back off of his torso.

He was deathly pale, his skin almost gray, and dark circles were under his eyes. I pushed him onto his back, shaking him again. His skin was ice cold.

"Get a healer!" I shouted to the guards, touching his face and neck. So cold.

He sucked in a rattling breath, which made my knees buckle in relief.

"Gunnar?" I cupped his face with both hands. "Can you open your eyes for me? Please?"

He wheezed again, his body shaking with the effort.

"Stay with me," I said, even though I wasn't sure if he heard me. "Help is on the way."

Healer witches arrived in what felt like ages. I got out of their way so they could attend to him, my entire body numb. The witches held their hands over him, talking rapidly to one another, before even more healers came in with a stretcher. They loaded him onto it and rushed away to the nearest healers' room.

I followed, but they shut me out and got to work. My stomach churned while anxiety pulsed through my veins to the point where sitting down was impossible. What had happened to him? Magical beings, especially Rulers and High Rulers, almost never got sick. Had he drugged himself?

I sweated underneath my coat as I paced, then ripped it off and put it on a chair a guard had gotten for me. Finally, a witch popped her head out of the room.

"He's stable and breathing more steadily," she said. "Would you like to come in?"

I nodded, the lump in my throat preventing me from speaking, and went inside. The room was separated into curtained off sections, and Gunnar was in the largest one at the far end. Healers came in and out with various tinctures and herbs in their hands.

I peered around the curtain and gasped. Gunnar somehow looked worse. Whatever spell they'd cast to keep him stable gave his skin an odd gray glow, like his insides had turned to stone and been lit up somehow. But he was breathing more steadily. That mattered.

"We've had to put him in a coma," one of the healers said to me.

"What happened to him?" I asked.

"We aren't sure yet. We're working on answers." The healer squeezed my shoulder and left me alone with him.

My whole body trembled as I sank into a chair next to his bed. He looked even younger than ever like this. So horrifyingly frail. A sob lurched up my throat so quickly that I nearly lost it. I pressed the heels of my hands to my forehead, taking steadying breaths. Gunnar drove me nuts most of the time, but as I'd tutored him, I'd seen the goodness in him.

Now he was close to death.

"Daria?" Oskar appeared in the corner of the curtained off area. Seeing him took away some of the tightness inside of my chest in an instant. "I came as soon as I could. Does anyone have any ideas about what happened?"

I shook my head, sniffing. "No. They put him in a coma temporarily until they can figure it out."

"My healers are incredibly capable," Oskar said, putting his big hand on my shoulder. The weight of it made me want to lean further into his touch. He'd wanted to comfort me this way yesterday, but I'd pulled away. I was glad I had because even this single point of contact was breaking my will to resist him.

"I know, but..." I swallowed to clear the lump in my throat, but it didn't help. Among the sadness and confusion came a rush of guilt. "What if he did this to himself?"

"Excuse me," one of the healers said, her hand on the curtain. "We'd like to try a few spells to see if we can figure out what happened to Ruler Gunnar."

Oskar held out his hand to help me to my feet, and I took it. My knees were still wobbly, so I was grateful for the help.

I let him go as soon as I was fully up and followed him out into the hallway.

"Here, come this way," Oskar said, pulling me down the hall and around the corner. He felt along the wall until he found a panel. He knocked on it as if it were a door, and it opened up to a small room.

"A secret room?" I asked.

"Yes. Only my guards and Freya have access. It was originally made as a safe room, but I've made it a space to get away for a few moments." He gestured for me to go ahead of him.

I walked down a short, dark hallway, which opened up into a very cozy room. One wall was taken up by a big bookshelf, and the other walls were painted a deep green shade. Charmed lights illuminated the space, making it feel warm instead of dungeon-like with its lack of windows. A big couch sat on the wall across from the bookshelf.

"Wow, this is nice," I said.

"It's one of my favorite spots, especially in winter." He rested a hand on my back and nudged me toward the couch. "Sit."

I sat, letting myself sink into the soft leather. He sat down as well, a few inches away from me. The couch wasn't small, but the size of the room and the darkness of it made me feel like we were hip to hip.

"Why do you think he did this to himself?" Oskar asked.

My stomach tightened again. "Think about it; he didn't want to be Ruler at all. He did well for a while, really pushed himself, then he just regressed. Maybe he decided it was too much for him, and he couldn't do it. And the only way out was this."

Oskar considered my words for a few moments, his brows furrowed. "I don't think he would do that, Daria."

"How do you know? What if I pushed him too hard?" I kicked off my boots and pulled my knees up to my chest.

"Daria." He squeezed my shoulder. "You can't blame yourself for this. Wasn't he feeling sick the day before? It's extremely rare, but Rulers can get sick sometimes. He was just making plans to visit home as soon as his training was done. I don't think he would try to kill himself."

I wiped my eye with the back of my hand, my skin coming away wet. How mortifying. I never cried. And the thought of Oskar of all people witnessing it made it even worse.

But he didn't point that out. He just moved his hand from my shoulder to the back of my neck, cupping and massaging it. The tension melted out of me in an instant.

"Don't feel guilty about this. You've done great work, and this has nothing to do with you," he said.

His deep voice relaxed me just as much as his hand did. He truly meant it, and the words got through to me. We had no idea what was happening to Gunnar, but I had no logical reason to believe it was all on me. My tears dried up, and I leaned into Oskar's touch. He took that as an invitation to pull me over until my head was resting on his muscled shoulder.

Being so close to him felt right, at least at that moment. He was warm and smelled like clean forest. His hand made big, sweeping strokes up and down my back, soothing me even further. We sat in silence that went from comfortable to charged in a different way over the course of a few minutes.

His hand was so huge that, in skimming up and down my back, his fingertips came close to the curve of my hip. I shifted to snuggle deeper into the couch, but I ended up getting closer to him instead. My heart started to flutter, then pounded when he turned to look at me.

I wasn't sure who started the kiss, but it happened. Unlike our first one, which was all fury and passion, this one was soft and slow. The gentleness of it overwhelmed me more than our angry kiss did, like he was stripping me layer by layer. I leaned into his touch, running my hand along the stubble on his cheeks.

He took the opportunity to deepen the kiss, pressing me onto my back and hovering above me. His lips trailed down the side of my neck as his warm hands slid underneath my sweater. I was already breathing fast, but the way he raked his teeth right above my sweater's neckline made me pant.

I pushed him backward to give me room to sit up and peel my sweater off. He did the same, tossing his aside next to mine. His body was even more gorgeous than I had imagined, thick muscle under smooth, fair skin. A light dusting of blond-brown hair trailed down his stomach and into his jeans, and I wanted to follow the path.

But he took over, leaving kisses down to my cleavage. Each deliberate press of his lips made my nipples ache for him to touch me there, but he avoided taking my bra off for the longest time.

Just before I exploded with frustration, he undid my bra and tossed it aside. He sucked in a breath as he studied me, like I was better than he'd imagined, too. The look made me pulse between my thighs, and he wasn't even touching me.

He cupped both of my breasts and leaned in for another kiss, this one dirtier and more intense than before. Our tongues slid against each other, our mouths perfectly in sync. I nipped his bottom lip, making him groan like I'd just stroked his cock.

"Oh, gods," I said against his mouth as he gently pulled at my nipples. I hadn't thought my breasts were particularly sensitive until now, but whatever he was doing changed my mind.

He brought his mouth to one of my nipples, sucking it in the same way he was playing with my other one. The rush of sensations made me soaked, tension winding up low in my belly. I squirmed under him, my leg brushing against the bulge in his pants. I tried to reach down to undo his belt buckle and get his pants off, but my arms were too short to reach.

"Isn't that uncomfortable?" I asked, brushing his erection with my leg again. The way his eyes fluttered closed made me grin, so I did it again.

"Daria," he said, his voice rough.

"What?" I smirked, continuing what I was doing.

In a flash, he flipped me onto my hands and knees, tugging my leggings and panties down to my ankles. He pushed my head down so my ass was up in the air and my center was exposed to him. I gasped into the throw pillow I'd landed on when he licked me, circling my clit but not fully touching it.

He held me still as he explored me with his mouth and tongue, tasting every part of me like I was the most delicious meal. My hips squirmed, and I tried to press back to get more contact, but his grip was iron, digging into my hips.

Eventually, he let go of one hip so he could undo his belt buckle, moaning against my wet flesh when he presumably pulled his cock out. I twisted as much as I could to see him. The top of his blond head was visible, along with his broad shoulders, but that was it. As if he had read my mind, he sat back and looked at me, his eyes hazy with lust.

He slowly pushed two fingers inside of me, making my toes curl and my hands grip the couch. I wanted to keep looking at him, to keep taking in his handsome face as he finger-fucked me, but my eyes squeezed shut. The pleasure was too intense, pushing all of my senses into overdrive—the scent and sound of my arousal, the sensation of his finger dragging across the sensitive spot inside of me.

My core fluttered around him, but he stopped before I came. My eyes popped open just in time for me to see him stroking his cock, my slickness lubricating him. The sight was going to be emblazoned in my brain forever. His broad, muscled shoulders, the way his forearm flexed as he ran his hand up and down his shaft.

"Please," I said, my voice breathy.

I didn't have to tell him twice. He lined himself up with my entrance and slid inside of me. He felt so big at this angle, filling me up so completely that my breath shortened.

"How do you feel this good, Daria?" he asked, his grip on my hips tightening again. "So tight."

I buried my face into the throw pillow again, my body trembling with pleasure already. His thrusting sped up, his hips smacking against my ass with the force of it. I assumed he had the room charmed to be soundproof, so I let go. I gasped and moaned, crying out when his cock hit just the right spot.

He leaned over me, his hips rocking against mine as he raked his teeth down my shoulder blade. One hand went from my hip to my clit, circling it with just enough pressure to set me off. I came so hard that I lost all control, pressing back against him and shuddering from head to toe.

My ears rang with the intensity of it, so I didn't catch what he said to me as he sped up. But he was close. His breathing was ragged, his face pressed to my back. After a few more hard pumps of his hips, he came with a sound so sexy that I knew I'd replay it in my head over and over again in the future.

He rested his hand on the back of the couch to gather himself, slowly pulling out. I flopped onto my hip, nearly falling off the couch, but he caught me. He pulled the cushions off the back of the couch to make room for himself and spooned himself behind me.

His warmth and size enveloped me like a set of armor, protecting me from the world. But the outside wasn't my biggest issue. I was still scared of whatever this was between us, as much as I tried to push that feeling away. My feelings were growing faster by the second, and the incredible sex wasn't slowing those down.

14

OSKAR

Daria and I stayed in my secret room for two more hours, going for another round with her on top. It was even better the second time. Just the memory of it made my cock ache, despite me trying to keep it in check. Her soft, full breasts bouncing as she rode me, the way she had sounded when she came...

I sighed and adjusted myself in my pants as subtly as I could without Freya noticing from her desk. I had much more pressing things to deal with now that Gunnar was out of commission.

The memory of Gunnar looking lifeless in the healers' room brought me back to reality. I didn't believe he'd done this to himself, like I'd told Daria. But the alternative was so much worse—that someone might have done this to him.

"I'm going to check on Gunnar," I said to Freya.

"Okay. I have everything under control here," she replied.

I left, my guards falling into step behind me. Gunnar had guards as well, though not as many as I did. In the flurry of activity going on around him, I hadn't questioned any of them yet. Then again, we didn't know what had happened to Gunnar. Having been the target of assassination attempts myself, my thoughts immediately went to him being attacked. I hoped I was wrong.

I found Daria standing outside of the healers' room, talking with one of the healers. Her brows were furrowed in concern as they chatted, her grip on the strap of her crossbody bag tight. Seeing her again after we had parted ways yesterday made me uneasy, to my surprise. But why? I thought that us breaking down and finally giving into the lust between us would get rid of that.

"Hello," I said to them.

"High Ruler." The healer bowed her head, as did Daria. "I was just updating Daria on Ruler Gunnar's status."

"Is he doing any better?" I asked.

The healer shook her head, her shoulders sagging. "No. But on the upside, he's not doing worse. He's still in his coma. We've done several spells on him to try to diagnose the issue, but nothing is working."

I frowned, crossing my arms over my chest. "How many people have worked with him?"

"As many as we have," she said, glancing over her shoulder as someone exited the room. All of the staff or members of my inner circle had been instructed to go to a healer in the nearest town if they needed help, so Gunnar had the healers' full attention. "Would you like to come in and see him?"

"Please."

The healer let us inside and guided us back to where Gunnar was. Seeing him again didn't lessen the shock of how bad he looked.

"Is he in pain?" His face was more tense than it was yesterday.

"We're not sure," another healer said, a warlock with a shaved head. "We've backed off on diagnostic spells for now, since using too much magic on him when he's this frail might do more harm than good."

Daria walked up to his bed and touched Gunnar's arm. His blue veins stood out against his skin even more starkly.

"He's burning up," she said.

"We know. He's had a fever off and on." The warlock healer ran a hand over his head, as if he were expecting hair to be there.

"What have you ruled out so far?" I asked.

The healer picked up a tablet and read off a long list of illnesses, some I'd heard of and others I hadn't. Daria's mouth pressed into a line, more out of concern than irritation with the healer.

"Do you think he could have been poisoned?" I demanded.

The warlock put the tablet back down on the counter next to him. "We can't know for sure. It looks like an illness coming from within, in my opinion, but again, we're still looking."

"Is there anyone else who specializes in healing bird shifters who could look at him?" Daria asked.

"We'd have to bring them in from elsewhere, but yes."

"Bring them in as soon as possible. Use portals to make it happen, as many as it takes."

"Of course." The healer bowed his head again. "I know just the healer. She's based in a town near the Bering Strait, so it may take some time to get her here."

"Bring her in as fast as possible." I turned to look at my guards.

"Yes, sir," the warlock answered.

"Good. Keep us updated. Daria, let's give them space to work."

I tried to keep my face neutral for the sake of everyone else as we walked out. But stealing one more look at Gunnar still yanked at something deep in my gut. I trusted my healers the way I trusted everyone else who worked under me, so I believed the warlock healer when he suspected it was an illness. But the fact that they still hadn't figured out what was wrong overnight was disturbing.

Daria and I left, walking side by side toward my office without speaking.

"He looks worse today," she finally said. "I hope this healer the warlock is bringing in helps."

"I know she will." I turned down a hall, and she followed me. "And if she doesn't, we'll keep looking for beings who can."

"I know." Daria took a deep breath and let it out, fiddling with the strap of her bag. "But how long could this go on?"

"I don't know."

We reached my office, and my guards opened the doors for us. Freya wasn't there, so I assumed she'd gone to talk to someone or to take a break. My office was much bigger than the little room where we'd had sex, but being alone with her in it shrunk the room down in my head.

Daria looked up at me, her cheeks flushed, as if she felt the same way. That uneasiness I'd felt when I first saw her today came rushing back, so I put space between us before I did something rash. My body protested—of course I wanted her, but what about everything else?

If she were one of my friends' aides, would I have felt more comfortable trying to start something more? Probably. But Filip's presence hovered in the back of my mind, pissing me off as if the real version of him had appeared. Daria was his friend and his second-in-command, just as I considered Freya a friend. And dating your enemy's friend didn't sit right with me.

Putting the fact that she was only here temporarily aside, being with Daria meant being around Filip more. And with that came centuries of baggage that no one could ignore, even with the undeniable feelings growing between us.

I studied her profile as she looked out the window—the angle of her feminine jaw, the smooth line of her nose, her elegant neck. I was physically attracted to her, but it was more than that. I wanted more than that. I wanted her sharp intelligence and moments of sass. I wanted more of those moments of us going back and forth, keeping me on my toes.

But what I wanted and what was best weren't always aligned, especially with everything going on. I needed to wait until the situation calmed down to even think about what our relationship was.

"Are you okay?" she asked.

"Hm?' I tucked my hands into my pockets. Had I been staring too blatantly? "As good as I can be given the circumstances. Why?"

She bit her bottom lip, glancing at a spot past my shoulder before looking back to me. "Nothing. We should figure out what to do while Gunnar is sick. And how to tell the Alphas about it, too."

"We should." I ran my hand over my face, making Daria smile. My heart squeezed in my chest at the sight of it, a bright spot in the darkness. "What?"

"You just captured exactly how I felt without saying a word." She took her bag off her shoulder. "Come on. Let's get to work."

15

———

DARIA

I never liked to say something was a mess without having an idea of how to clean it up, but...

"This is a mess," I said to Oskar, looking over the report that Freya had put together early this morning. "And now we have even more of a mess on top of it."

"That bad?" He slid a hand across my shoulders and left it there, leaning over me to look at the report. The warmth of his touch soothed me even through the barrage of bullshit that we were dealing with.

"Yes." No need to sugarcoat it. "The crime among falcon shifters across the region is way, way up, even in the packs where their Alpha is still in place. Even in the areas where we've sent temporary help for packs without Alphas that are struggling. They'd like their leaders back. Or at least they'd like to know where they are."

Oskar sighed and leaned against the edge of the desk, tucking his hands into his pockets. "I'm not sure they'd like the Alphas that they have right now."

"I know."

We had worked together through the night to figure out what to do with Gunnar out of commission, and now we were trying to figure out what to do with all of the Alphas. We poured over each of the reports that members of Oskar's inner circle had put together during their training, trying to find some bright spots there. The positives in the reports were total stretches, like "attended the session today" and "didn't speak out against me today."

The Alphas didn't want to follow the rules that were in place so that they didn't abuse their power. They didn't like the fact that they couldn't just barge into rabbit shifter territory, which was how the past wave of Alphas had been put to death—a fact they knew but apparently didn't care about. As Ulla had said, according to one of her reports, "regular rabbits are our prey—why should we bother respecting rabbit shifters?"

Luckily, the member of the inner circle who had created her report said he had managed to talk her down from that. At least for now.

I checked the time. We'd hardly slept, something that was wearing more on me than it was on Oskar, but the longer we waited to tell the Alphas about Gunnar's condition, the worse off we probably were. Or at least I assumed so.

"Should we even tell them?" I asked, curling one leg up underneath me. I'd kicked off my boots a while ago since we hadn't left the room in hours. "They've only met him in controlled circumstances back when he was on his good streak, so maybe we could keep them in the dark for longer. They don't really know how he is as Ruler anyway."

"Yeah, but that's good and bad." He reached over to pull another chair next to me. "They don't know him, so not seeing him for a few more days wouldn't be amiss. But that also means that they don't trust him, and the more that mistrust grows, the more problems we'll have down the line."

"You're right." I ran both hands over my face and yawned. "Gods, I need a boost."

"Take a nap, Daria," he said, reaching over and squeezing my thigh. "You've been up for a long time."

"I know, but we still have so much work to do." I yawned again, expecting him to yawn as well. But nope, he looked just as awake and handsome as ever. "How much sleep do you even need in one night?"

"Eh, three hours, maybe." He shrugged, turning my chair so I was facing him and we were knee to knee. "But you need more. And you've been putting in a lot of work—"

"There's still—"

"Daria." The deep timbre of his voice shut me up instantly, making my thighs clench together. "Rest, or else."

"Or else what?" I asked. Even in my exhausted state, I craved him again. We hadn't had the chance to even touch each other all that much since we had slept together. But gods, this was not the time.

"Or I'll do this." He scooped me up, making me yelp, and brought me over to the couch.

"Put me down," I said, my voice weak. Being in his arms, snuggled against his chest, was criminally comfortable.

He finally put me down on the couch on the far side of his office and pulled my feet up so I was laying down. Then, he unearthed a blanket from a chest nearby and tossed it over me.

"I'll handle our plan while you get at least an hour of rest," he said. The command in his voice told me the case was closed.

I glared at him, which only made him give me a cocky smile, like he was reveling in his small victory. I hated how much that turned me on.

He dimmed the lights in my area of his office, which put me out in moments. I slipped into such a deep sleep that I was disoriented when I woke up.

"How long was I out?" I asked, my voice raspy.

"For two hours," he said from across the room. He was at his desk, still typing away. "Go back to sleep."

"No." I adjusted my clothes from where I'd rolled around in my sleep and got up. "What have you gotten done?"

"I've taken a closer look at the entire situation and gotten Freya's opinion," he said, turning to face me. "We should tell them individually and take a different approach with each one. Waiting until they hear from someone else will break their trust in us."

"Okay." I rubbed my eyes and sat down at the chair next to his. "What approach will we take?"

"It seems like Klaus and Artem are the most reactive and aggressive," he said, pushing a printed document toward me. "So, they might see Gunnar being in a coma as a chance to somehow get ahead and get more power. Pasha is the least problematic of all of them, so he'll be the easiest. Ulla and Annelli won't want to play by the rules, so if we tell them to do something directly, they might resist."

I skimmed the document, which outlined the plan. We had to tell them all at once, so my inner circle was going to help. Someone would tell Klaus and Artem that Oskar was the interim Ruler, since he was the only being they couldn't overpower. As for Annelli and Ulla, someone else would tell them that he was sick, but we were managing his duties temporarily—hopefully, they wouldn't push back. And Pasha was going to get the regular truth. At least one of them wasn't an issue.

Still, we had no idea what their reactions were going to be.

"Great," I said, looking up at him. "I guess we have to give this a shot. We don't have much of a choice."

"You're sure you're fine with this?" he asked.

I blinked, studying his face. He was asking genuinely, like he trusted me completely. Filip had placed that kind of trust in me since we'd worked together for so long. The fact that we'd gone from butting heads to this filled my belly with a strange warmth. All I wanted from Oskar was to feel like he respected my centuries of experience, and now we were there, plus some.

The sex wasn't the thing that had pushed us over into this, was it? No, it didn't feel like it was just the new sexual direction our relationship had taken. We had hardly touched this whole time. Plus, he was High Ruler, not some random male who made decisions based on who he was sleeping with. Certain leaders, yes. But he'd been High Ruler for so long that I doubted he was one of them.

"I'm fine," I finally replied.

"Okay." He cupped the back of my neck.

"Yeah, just more tired than I thought," I admitted.

"Mm." He started massaging my neck the way he had the night we'd slept together. It was just as potent as it had been then, making me melt into his touch.

"You're too good at that," I said. "If you keep going, we're never going to get anything done."

"I know." He gave my neck one more squeeze. "I'll go ahead and task some inner circle members to talk to Ulla, Annelli, Pasha, and Artem. And we'll talk to Klaus."

I finger-combed my hair back into place. "The hardest one for us?"

"Yep."

"Let's go, then."

The Alphas weren't supposed to be in sessions with members of Oskar's inner circle, so we hoped to catch them in their quarters. Luckily, Klaus was in his. The guard outside of his door announced our presence, and Klaus came to the door. He was wearing a flannel pajama set, his hair rumpled like he'd been in bed.

"Hello, High Ruler. Hello, Daria." He stepped back to let us in.

We stepped inside. His quarters were set up a lot like mine—a large bedroom with a bed and two side tables, a living room, and a door that I assumed led to an office space the way mine did. He led us to the living room space, and we sat down around the coffee table.

"We have some news for you," Oskar said, sitting back into the couch. "Ruler Gunnar is ill, and he's been put into a medically-induced coma for now."

Klaus blinked, his expression blank. "What happened?"

"The healers are investigating," I said. "We'll tell everyone what's happened once we know more."

Klaus rubbed at one of his eyes, as if he were still tired. "Who's in charge for now? One of us Alphas?"

Of course he went straight to that.

"I am," Oskar said.

Klaus bit back an answer, reconsidered what he was going to say, then said, "Sir, you're not a falcon shifter."

"I'm the High Ruler, and I rule over all the beings in this region.

Remember your place." Oskar's voice was hard, just as it should have been.

Klaus swallowed hard, looking away.

"At least it's not her," he grumbled, as if I wasn't right there.

Oskar was across the coffee table in an instant, his hand around Klaus' throat. Klaus' eyes widened, his face going red as Oskar slowly applied pressure. The Alpha clawed at Oskar's hand, but Oskar was much stronger than he was.

"Listen," Oskar growled. "She's a thousand times more qualified to be the Ruler than you are. Don't disrespect her ever again. Understood?"

Klaus went pale, mouthing *yes, sir* over and over again until Oskar finally let go. My heart squeezed at his defense of me. I was never going to be Ruler in my own region, but knowing he thought I could do it was a boost to my confidence.

"Sorry," Klaus said, clearing his throat and straightening his t-shirt. "Do the others know? About Gunnar?"

"They're being told right now."

"Even Artem?" Klaus' voice darkened.

Were they still upset at each other for the fight they'd had over Klaus' mate?

"Yes, even him." Oskar rested his hands on his knees like he was about to get up. "Do you have any more questions?"

"Yeah, one more thing. What happens if Gunnar doesn't pull through?"

The question was innocent enough—I would have wondered as well. But the edge in his voice made the question feel anything but innocuous.

"Then the Magic will decide who's next." Oskar stood. "Your training will continue as usual."

"Thank you for the visit, High Ruler." Klaus stood as well. He hardly acknowledged me as we left, the asshole.

Once we rounded the corner away from Klaus' quarters, I said, "We should increase the security around Gunnar."

"Agreed." Oskar pulled his phone from his pocket, presumably to notify his head of security to put more guards near Gunnar. "I didn't like his attitude."

"Me either." I sighed. "The last thing we need is for one of the Alphas to try to kill him."

"We have it under control." He sounded so confident, reassuring me. I stepped closer to him, the urge to take his hand rushing up inside of me. We made a pretty good team now that we weren't pushing against each other every step of the way. I just hoped that it was enough to help us ride through these waves.

16

OSKAR

Even though I needed much less sleep than the average wolf shifter, I still enjoyed it. I liked it even more when I woke up with Daria in my arms. She was so small, yet sturdy. Muscular, but with softness that felt just right.

I pulled her closer, resting my chin on top of her head. Her hair smelled like vanilla and coconut, but not in a way that was too cloying for my heightened senses. All of her was just right. After a long day of dealing with the Alphas and Gunnar's health situation, we hit a point where we didn't have anywhere to go in our investigations. So, I'd brought her back to my bedroom, and we hadn't slept as much as we should have.

I opened my eyes and checked the clock on the far wall. We had a little bit of time before we had to start the day.

I ran my hands down her middle, cupping her between her thighs. She stirred but didn't wake up fully yet.

"Daria," I murmured in her ear, grinding my hardening cock against her ass.

"Yeah?" She yawned. She pressed back against me, making me harden even more, and shifted her legs so my fingers could slip between her folds. With just a few circles of her clit, she was wet.

She rolled over to face me, throwing a leg over my hips to give my hand more space. I bit back a groan when she grasped my cock, getting me fully hard without much effort. We worked each other up in tandem, her breath hot against my chest. I rolled onto my back, kissing her as if we had all day. Then, she slid onto me in one smooth move.

She pulled me close, so our bodies were flush against each other as I started to move. The closeness of our bodies and the sound of her ragged breath in my ear made it feel just as intimate as it would have if we were making eye contact. As much as I enjoyed that, I wanted to see her ride me.

I pressed her back until she was sitting up and rested my hands behind my head. She gave me a small smirk in response but didn't say anything. I sat up to kiss her again, but she took my hand instead, kissing my palm, then the golden sun tattoo on my inner wrist that signified my High Ruler status, and up my arm until she reached my lips.

The gesture was so simple, but it pulled at something deep inside me in a way I couldn't describe. But it was good and exactly right.

She wrapped her legs around me as we kissed, and the change took me deeper inside of her, swallowing me fully in her warmth. The sensations were overwhelming so soon after waking up that I reached the edge after just a few minutes of being inside of her. Daria was right there with me, clenching around me and biting down on my shoulder.

She came before me, pulling my climax from me from the force of it. I saw stars, the breath leaving my lungs in a rush. I braced myself on my hands so I wouldn't crush her, then flopped on my back next to her.

"Morning," she said, a smile in her voice.

"Morning." I sat up on one elbow and took her in.

I loved the way her hair was rumpled in the morning. The sight of her here, bleary eyed and loose, was too easy to get used to. The worries that I'd successfully staved off overnight came rushing back. We had to go outside and face the real world eventually—a real world where our relationship was strained by our past and now all of this conflict in our present.

"I should get dressed," Daria said, sliding out of bed. "I have to handle a few things before dealing with the Alphas and their training."

"Okay." I wasn't sure whether to get up and join her or wait. Ultimately, I waited.

She quickly dressed, throwing her coat on to hide the fact that she was wearing yesterday's clothes, and left with a shy wave. No hug, no kiss. Fine. I was sure she had the same reservations as I did about us becoming closer.

I dressed and went to my office, an attendant delivering breakfast to me. Freya arrived not long after, her eyes weary, even though the day had barely started.

"What's wrong?" I asked.

She held up her tablet for a second before sitting down at her desk. "I have some things to report to you. Give me a moment."

I watched her tap on the tablet, her expression darkening by the moment. Finally, she looked up and sighed.

"There have been some falcon shifter riots over in Sweden," she said. "I just got word from the Alpha there about it. And I've gotten reports from the temporary aid we sent to the packs without Alphas that their populations are uneasy, too. They feel like they don't have leadership, so some are trying to snatch the opportunity for nefarious purposes."

I took a long drink of my tea as if it were alcohol. I wished it had the same effect.

"How bad were the riots?" I asked.

"Not terrible. The Alpha has been on high alert, given everything that's been going on, so they took care of it before it got out of hand. Some property was damaged, but no one was seriously injured." She looked down again at her tablet. "But I'm not sure how much longer we can keep the peace."

"Punishing all of the shifters involved in the riots is a good start. Have them arrested."

"Of course, sir. I'll have that done right away," Freya said. "Aside from that, we might have to expedite the training process and see if we can continue it while the Alphas are back with their packs."

"Maybe." I pushed back from my desk and started pacing, my drink in hand. "The only one I'd feel comfortable sending back is Pasha since he's in the right mindset. The others are still too rebellious. Daria and I increased the security outside of Gunnar's room because of how threatening Klaus sounded when we told him about Gunnar's illness."

Freya blinked. "Really?"

"Yes, really. If we let him go back and didn't send him with the right kind of help to keep him in line, we might end up with another situation with rabbit shifters or worse." I stopped near the window. The sky was gray, the clouds so heavy that they hung low, giving the landscape a hazy look. "The others aren't much better."

My stomach tightened, but I kept my face neutral. All I wanted for my region was peace. How far would all of this unrest go? What if I let more people die because I wasn't doing enough?

"Would you like to take a walk and talk about it? I'd like to get some tea." Freya stood up and smoothed her hands down her sweater dress.

"Sure."

Her asking to get tea was her code for talking me down from the ledge. As unnerving as it was for someone to see through my High Ruler façade, I appreciated it from her. I needed my second-in-command to be an extension of myself.

We put our coats on and went outside, taking one of the wide paths across the grounds of the palace. In spring, it was lush and green, but with it getting deeper into fall, the path had lost its color.

"Are you distressed about this situation because of what happened before?" Freya asked. We both knew what she was referencing.

"Yes. But it's different." I finished my tea and looked to one of my guards, who trailed behind us at a distance to give us privacy. She rushed up, took the mug, and went back to her place. "We've been trying so damn hard to get everything and everyone up to standard, but things keep going awry."

"But we're doing the best we can," Freya pointed out. "You know that. And not everything is awful. Gunnar isn't getting any worse, for instance. The odds are good that he'll recover once the healers figure out what happened. We can't control for every variable in every situation."

I sighed. She was right. After I had let my hubris get in the way of protecting the wolf shifters in my region all those centuries ago, I'd tried to grab onto every possible problem and bend it to my will. But ruling that way was asking for trouble. Like she said, some problems were always going to be out of our control.

"And Daria..." I said.

Just saying her name made the stress filling my chest contort and tighten, as if it wasn't sure whether to grow or relax. The circumstances around us were a prime example of how I couldn't control everything, but my brain refused to apply Freya's words to that.

"What about her?" Freya asked.

"We would have been in even deeper trouble if she wasn't here," I said.

"And?"

I turned onto a side path that went toward the palace compound's main kitchen. "And what?"

"I'm not completely unaware of how you two have grown closer, you know." Freya's lips quirked up in a smile. "One day, you were ripping each other's heads off, and the next, you two were working together perfectly."

I cleared my throat, not wanting to look her in the eye. "I know."

"Isn't that a good thing?" she replied. "Having your relationship be much less volatile?"

Freya was married to a bear shifter named Mikhail, so she always had someone in her corner, even though he traveled frequently for his work. Instead of letting that blind her to the relationship problems that single beings had, she used her experience to give good advice. I hadn't had significant feelings for a female in ages, so talking about it felt awkward. But Freya was the closest ally I had, and I needed to talk to someone about it.

"It would be an amazing thing if we didn't have all of the baggage from the past and if she wasn't Filip's second-in-command," I said. "We've gotten over our past differences, but do you really see me and Filip even tolerating each other? How am I supposed to be with her if she has to be close to my greatest enemy all the time? And what if Filip somehow turns her against me?"

"Daria is way too independent to let someone sway her opinions that easily, especially if she has strong feelings for you," Freya said, slowing to a stop and allowing my guards to open the doors to the main dining hall for us.

"True, but that doesn't change the fact that Filip exists. And she'll have to go back to him sometime. She's been his second-in-command for centuries. She won't drop that role for a relationship."

I stopped talking as we walked through the dining hall, guests stopping to bow their heads toward me in respect. The entire kitchen staff did the same when we entered, and someone quickly made Freya a fresh cup of tea. They were baking scones for later as well, so I took one to eat while we walked. I didn't continue our conversation until we were outside again, a good distance from the dining hall.

"I'm not sure how to proceed with Daria," I said. "I have feelings for her, which isn't something I ever thought I'd say, and she feels for me. At least from what I can tell. But the issues we're facing are very real, and we have so much going on. I don't want to make a mistake here, too."

"Your fears make sense," she said. She took a turn onto a less-traveled path, one that cut across the courtyard near the guest quarters to get back to the main building of the palace faster. "But you don't have to decide exactly where you stand with her right now, especially since other things are taking priority. Maybe you can continue being close until all of the Alphas are trained and Gunnar is better. Then you can decide what to do."

"I suppose that's what I'll have to do." Her plan was logical, but knowing that didn't take away my anxiety right away.

"Here," Freya said, coming to a stop and opening her arms. "You'll be fine."

No one was around aside my guards, who had taken an oath of secrecy regarding my matters, so I hugged her back. Freya loved to give everyone hugs, but she rarely gave them to me anymore. It was comforting, almost maternal. As much power and authority came naturally to me as High Ruler, having someone who always had my back and who I trusted entirely was priceless.

"Thanks," I murmured, letting her go.

"Any time." She smiled, but it quickly turned to a frown. She dug into her pocket and checked her phone. "I got an alert from the healer. They have news about Gunnar."

"Come on," I said, turning to go to the healers' room.

We rushed over. I pushed past the guards to open the doors to his room myself, hoping to see Gunnar sitting up. But no—he was still in bed, his eyes closed. The healers next to him whipped around and bowed in deference.

"Thank you for coming so quickly, High Ruler," a warlock healer said.

"Of course. Is he okay? What happened?"

The warlock glanced to a fae healer, who nodded.

"My initial thoughts were incorrect," he said. "We know that Ruler Gunnar has been poisoned, but we have no idea by what or by who."

The room went so silent that Gunnar's slight wheezing floated through the room.

"Poisoned," I repeated.

"Yes. We're hard at work figuring out what it could be, but poisons are a big area of study," the warlock said. "And whatever this is, it must be rare. We'll have to do a lot of digging to find out what it is."

"I'll have members of my inner circle look into it as well." I glanced at Gunnar, who had some patchy stubble along his cheeks from being in a bed for days. "We need to find answers in case his assailant is targeting anyone else."

17

DARIA

I had planned to go to Oskar's office after I came back to my quarters to handle a few things for Filip that only I could do, but I was still in my attached office, staring blankly out the window. The knot in my throat hadn't gone away since I'd seen Oskar and Freya hugging across the courtyard. I nearly missed seeing them, but I'd caught them at the last second.

They had hugged. That was it. But it had looked so intimate that every ugly insecurity I'd tried to banish came rushing back.

Why did I get my hopes up about Oskar? Freya was stunning, much more statuesque and traditionally attractive than I was. Plus, she was his second-in-command. The relationship between a High Ruler and his second-in-command was always close, as they were often the only being who they allowed to challenge them or see their vulnerable side. Having a romantic relationship wasn't out of the picture.

I'd hoped I'd get that with Filip before Mylee came along. I saw him at his best and his worst, seeing past the aloof yet powerful exterior he showed everyone else. But he never saw me as more than that. Seeing him happy with Mylee made the sting of rejection less painful, but never enough to forget the centuries I had spent pining after him.

I sighed and walked around my desk to sit down again. How many times was I going to be in this situation, where I felt for someone who didn't have eyes for me and me alone? I'd seen countless couples mate bond, and the way they acted with each other made my heart ache with envy. Mate bonds were rare, so I never expected to have one. But I wanted love, at least. To know that I was someone's first choice.

I closed my eyes and pulled myself together. It was a hug. Not a kiss. Not an open confession of love. I had no idea what it truly meant for them.

But it only reminded me of how many obstacles Oskar and I had between us. Our backgrounds, the distance between Florida and Iceland, and all of the problems I was here to fix. And maybe he needed the sex to blow off steam in a stressful time. Maybe that tender look he had given me this morning was just a post-sex high.

Being with him was too much of a risk, and the realization was a knife to the heart. Even if the hug were nothing, it didn't change the fact that we were never going to work.

My phone buzzed on my desk, and I grabbed it, thinking it was Filip. But it was Oskar. Lovely.

"Hello?"

"We have news about Gunnar," he said. "Can you come to my office, please?"

"Of course, I'll be there soon." His tone wasn't easy to read, but at least he didn't sound too upset. My desire for news about Gunnar outweighed any feelings I had toward him.

I rushed to his office and found him alone, aside from one of his attendants near the door. My stomach knotted up so tightly that it took my breath away. Seeing him felt so much worse than I thought it would. The light coming in from the window glinted off his blond hair, making it look like gold, and he was wearing the sweater I loved on him—dark blue, soft, and clinging to all of his muscles in just the right way.

"Daria," he said, coming toward me.

"What's the news with Gunnar?" I asked, keeping my distance.

Oskar glanced behind me at his attendant, who left the room. I wished he hadn't dismissed her. Now the office felt even smaller. Thankfully, he perched on the edge of his desk instead of coming closer to me.

"He was poisoned," Oskar said, his eyebrows furrowing.

"By what? Or who?" I asked. "How is that possible?"

"They don't know yet. And we don't know how, either." He pushed up the sleeves of his sweater, revealing the golden sun tattoo on his inner wrist. Seeing it made my stomach lurch. I'd kissed it this morning as I rode him. The memory was jarring. "But we interviewed all of his guards, and they didn't see anything. One of them has to be lying."

My heart pounded, blood rushing in my ears. Had Klaus gotten to him before we had even talked? Or were his guards lying? The latter didn't make sense to me—everyone on Oskar's security team was dedicated to their job. Then again, they were loyal to Oskar, not to Gunnar. I hadn't met all of his guards, but at least two were falcon shifters. Were they in on this?

Oskar approached me again, putting a hand on my shoulder and sliding it to the back of my neck. I stepped away and went to the window, ignoring the confused look on his face.

"We're trying to figure out what happened," he said. "I have the healers on it, as well as members of my inner circle. Are you all right?"

I swallowed the lump in my throat. "I'm fine, aside from the fact that Gunnar was poisoned, and we have no idea who did or why."

"Then why won't you let me touch you?" He came up behind me, backing me up against the window. "You were completely fine this morning."

His body was a wall, taking up my field of vision. I had no reason to lie to him, and I didn't want to leave him wondering what had happened.

"I just realized that we can't work," I said, looking him right in the eye, even though it hurt to do so.

Seeing the confusion flash into his pale blue eyes hurt even more. "What do you mean?"

"We never made any commitments to each other," I said.

"It doesn't take a commitment to know we were going somewhere, Daria." He gave me space, and the extra air let me release some of the tension in my shoulders.

"I know we were, but we shouldn't. Do you really think that we can just put aside our past and just be together?" I asked. "We hated each other just a few weeks ago. For *centuries*."

"And clearly, we don't now." He dug his hand into his hair, looking at me as if he'd never seen me before. "Or at least I thought so. I know we have some history and some hurdles, but can't we just see where this goes?"

The pleading tone in his voice tore down my first layer of defenses, but I still had more protecting my heart.

"See where this goes?" I echoed. "The fact of the matter is that I'm Filip's second-in-command, and he's your biggest rival. I have to go home once all of this is over. My loyalties lie with him."

"He has a mate."

"I know that." I crossed the room since standing still made me antsy. "But I'm not talking about that. I'm talking about my work. I'm not easily replaced in Filip's inner circle. And even if we tried something long distance, how am I supposed to get close to someone who my closest friend hates? It's not like you can pretend he doesn't exist and vice versa."

"I don't know, Daria." He let go of his hair and sat down in a leather armchair next to one of his bookcases. "Maybe we could come to some agreement or truce."

He was grasping at straws. Seeing the cracks in his armor, the vulnerability in his eyes, made me feel naked as well. I hoped my outside didn't match how obliterated I felt on the inside, but I doubted my feelings were tucked neatly away.

"An agreement. You want to make up with Filip so we can keep having sex?" I said.

"This isn't just sex for me. I care about you." He sounded so sure, but I didn't believe him. "Let's wait until we get the Alphas trained and figure out what happened with Gunnar to make this decision. When this is all over, Filip and I can work out our differences, and we can continue to see each other."

I looked down at the rings on my fingers, which I twisted around and around.

"I can't do that," I said, my voice raspy from trying to hold back tears. "I really don't see it working out. I know Filip more than I know anyone else. I doubt he'll agree to that kind of truce or whatever you'd like to call it."

"Even if agreeing to get along with me would make you happy?" Storminess came into his eyes for the first time. "Actually, yeah, that seems like the kind of asshole he is."

"That's what I mean." I laughed, even though nothing was funny. "You'll never get along."

He didn't respond—he just looked at me. The cold, flat look in his eyes unnerved me. Was I judging him that harshly? I didn't know. But our talk had cemented my decision.

"I'm going to look into some possible poisons that Gunnar was exposed to," I said instead.

"I already have members of my inner circle on it."

"Then you have one more." I buttoned my coat. "I came here to train Gunnar, and the sooner he's back on the mend, the sooner I can finish my job and go home."

"Fine." He stood up and crossed the office in a few long-legged strides. "Report back to me with what you have."

He yanked the door open and gestured for me to get out. I glared at him for a beat before stepping out, my heart breaking into smaller pieces the farther I walked away from him.

18

OSKAR

I wanted to throw something across my office, but I held myself together. What the hell had just happened with Daria? We were completely fine this morning, then she'd made a complete turn away from me.

I tried to go back to my work, but my thoughts were consumed with her. She'd brought up the very points that I'd brought up to Freya, but instead of choosing to move past those fears, she had caved into them.

Had I misread her? Or the situation? She wasn't the most expressive female, but I saw the softness in her eyes and felt how good we were together, even if it was brief. Did I do something or say something to make her change her mind so suddenly?

How had I let myself fall for her in the first place? My gut instinct to stay away from her was right, even though my heart was wrong. Very wrong. I had offered to end my rivalry with Filip for her, and she had pushed me away.

My phone rang, and for a moment, I feared it was Daria. But it was worse—it was Anja, the rabbit shifter Ruler. I'd told her to call me directly if she ever had any concerns, but throwing another problem onto the pile was going to break me soon.

"Hello?" I stood by the window, leaning against the frame.

"High Ruler, hello. I hope I haven't caught you at a bad time," Anja said. Her usually soft voice had an edge to it that put me on high alert.

"No, this is fine. How can I help you?"

"I appreciate the aid that you've sent in light of our meeting, but it hasn't been enough," she said. "We've had more attacks over in the eastern side of the region by falcon shifters who claimed they thought they were regular rabbits. Luckily, nobody was killed, thanks to your team, but there were serious injuries."

I closed my eyes, my grip on my phone tightening. Those falcon shifters were blatantly lying. Every shifter could tell the difference between a regular animal and a shifter version of that animal. My wolf form was far bigger and stronger than a normal wolf, and rabbit shifters were much bigger and more physically resilient than regular rabbits.

"I'm sorry to hear that," I said, even though the words didn't fully express my anger at this whole situation.

"I know you do, and I know you care," she said, her voice softening to the tone I was used to. "But what else can we do?"

"I'll increase the security. And I'll send a team to apprehend the offending falcon shifters for punishment to set an example. I won't tolerate this violence," I said. "The new Alphas are still being trained, and soon, they'll help keep things in order."

Training out their distaste for rabbit shifters was going to be harder, but she didn't need to know that.

"Thank you," she sighed.

"You're welcome. I promise I'll handle this." I wished Gunnar were awake to deal with this, just for practice. It was the type of situation he would have to handle as the new falcon shifter Ruler. "I'll have more help sent as soon as we end this call."

"Thank you, High Ruler."

She hung up, and I did what I said I'd do. It only took me a few minutes, which put me back in my terrible mood about Daria. I attended to some other things under the falcon shifter Ruler's purview to distract myself, but it only made me worry about Gunnar. What if we never figured out what had poisoned him, and the healers had to keep him in a coma indefinitely? Some High Ruler had probably dealt with the issue before, but I wasn't one of them. I didn't want it to come to that.

Being in my office felt like being in a cage, so I went to the library, where members of my inner circle were hard at work looking into various poisons. Stacks of books were piled up on every available surface, certain pages glowing where the librarian witch, Ivanna, had found pertinent information.

"Hello, sir," Dimitri, a bear shifter who had been in my inner circle for centuries, said.

"How's the research going?" I asked, studying the book on top of the stack next to him.

"It's tedious. It's like Ruler Gunnar has every symptom of every poison out there." Dimitri closed his book, which looked tiny in his huge hands. "And there are a lot of poisons out there."

"I can see that." I glanced down the table, then at my inner circle. "Is anyone having any luck?"

"I might be," Ivanna said. I went to her side of the table to see what she was doing. She had a list of all of the information the spells had revealed, including what was in his blood, next to her books. "The poison is probably something that would affect any shifter, not just a bird shifter. And since his guards never saw anyone unusual approach him or try to enter his room, he either ingested it somehow, or if dark magic was involved, someone may have used a spell to poison him from a distance."

I rested my hands on the table. "Did any witches or warlocks feel any traces of dark magic around him or his quarters?"

"I've tasked someone to check," Dimitri said. "And we have people interviewing the kitchen staff about what was served the day he was found."

"Good." They always anticipated the next steps, so I had nothing to worry about on that front

But I needed something to do, or I'd feel useless, and by extension, powerless. And I never wanted to feel that way.

"Hand me some books," I told Ivanna, sitting down. "There's a lot to get through."

She handed me a stack of four heavy, ancient books. I read over the document she was referencing and started my own research.

The names of the poisons and the effects of them blended together in my head the more I read and the more I had to cross-reference other books. The books were tedious on top of that, written for reference and not for reading.

I had meals brought in for everyone, so we didn't have to stop working. I was moments from losing my mind after reading what felt like the same piece of information for the fiftieth time until I saw something different—a reference to a book that wasn't on the table.

"Ivanna, grab this book for me."

She came over to see what I was referencing and frowned.

"It should be out here. The call number says it's one from the ancient plants database." She ran her finger along the text, then disappeared into the stacks. She came back empty-handed a few minutes later. "It's not here."

She held her hands out toward the books, presumably doing a spell, but the books on the table fluttered open, then closed.

"No one has it?" I asked.

"Have you seen it, Astrid?" Ivanna asked her assistant, a meek rabbit shifter named Astrid.

Astrid's cheeks colored, and she kept her eyes on the books in front of her. "I haven't, no."

"Let me try a different spell," Ivanna said. She went into the stacks. A breeze blew through the library, and she finally came back with a book in her arms. Still, she had a frown on her face.

"What's wrong?" I asked.

"The book is here, but the information is gone." She opened the book to the proper page.

It was wiped clean, like it had never been printed with the rest of the book in the first place. I took the book from her and paged through it to see if any more pages had been removed. The rest of the book was fine.

"I don't know what happened, sir," Ivanna said, the blood draining out of her face.

"Can you find out what did?" I handed the book back to her.

"Yes, with some help, I think." She looked down at the book, her eyes wide. "I'll get right on it."

"Good." The rest of my inner circle had stopped their work, glancing at each other, the tension in the room high. "I think we've found a lead, then."

Someone didn't want us to find the answer, but that only made me want to figure it out more.

19

———

DARIA

Oskar's inner circle had taken over the library doing research into what might have poisoned Gunnar, but I was able to ask Ivanna to duplicate a few of the books for me in the meantime.

The process took time, so I paced around and organized my things while I waited. Eventually, someone knocked on my door, and I rushed to get it. It was Astrid, Ivanna's assistant. She had a rabbit-like look to her—a cute, slightly upturned nose and big, sweet eyes.

"I have the books you requested," she said, pushing the cart forward. "I have to take the cart back, unfortunately, so I'll have to drop them off for you. Ivanna wrote a note explaining what everything was."

"Thank you. We can put them in my office."

I stepped aside, and she pushed the cart into the room, turning the corner to my office space. I helped her pull the books off the shelf, stacking them on my desk. Most of them were obvious duplicates, books with plain outsides and the names etched into the sides, but one was ancient. I picked it up, running my hand over the cover.

"Oh, um..." Astrid stared at the book in my arms.

"What?" I asked, looking at the title. The book was about transmutation, turning certain elements into others. "Am I not allowed to have this?"

"You can," she said with a nervous smile. I tried to soften my expression as to not make her any more nervous. My bad mood was making an unwanted appearance at the wrong being. "Do you need anything else?"

"No, I'm fine. Thank you."

I opened the door for her, and she left me alone with thousands of pages of information to go over.

I barely had enough space for my laptop and a notepad. I was glad for this many distractions. I didn't want to think about anything but finding what and who had poisoned Gunnar.

Finding out the poison he had been dosed with was the fastest path to finding who had done it. Or at least I hoped so. Poisons were sourced from particular locations, so unless someone was growing it illegally, I'd be able to follow the path back to where it'd come from and find out who had bought it.

I rubbed my eyes with the back of my hand and yawned. When was the last time I'd slept? I wasn't sure. The last good night of sleep I'd gotten had been with Oskar.

Ugh.

I went back to my research, diving deep into each of the books. All of Gunnar's symptoms were so general, the kind that fit a number of poisons. Doing all of this work on my own was a little foolish, yes, but I didn't want to be around anyone at the moment. And I'd asked them to send me the most important updates on everything and trusted them to do so, so I wasn't very guilty for giving myself space away from Oskar and others.

Homesickness crashed over me, making my stomach ache. Oskar's inner circle was great, and everyone had been welcoming, but it wasn't the same as being home. I'd known everyone back in Florida for centuries, and they were family to me. And I missed the sun and warmth.

I pushed away from my desk and stretched my legs. I'd been cooped up for way too long. I needed to shift and get some air.

I opened a window and shifted, flying outside. Being in falcon form was warmer than my human form, even when I was at higher altitudes and the wind was blowing back in my face.

I took off, soaring above the palace and across a plateau toward the mountains in the distance. The view was stunning, more than making up for the slight chill in the air. The only sounds were from nature, the regular birds chirping, the crashing of waterfalls, the bubbling of streams. I'd been cooped up inside for too long when I needed to be out here, taking in the serenity I'd been missing.

I flew aimlessly, sometimes diving down to hunt small animals but mostly just letting the air carry me. I flew through fjords, above glaciers, and just above the ocean. I was finally able to shut my brain off for a while. I'd been so preoccupied with the cold that I'd missed out on a lot of opportunities to explore how beautiful it all was.

I turned, heading back toward the palace as it got darker. On my way back, I spotted a massive white wolf shifter below, and my heart tugged. What was Oskar doing out here? I peeled off to the side, avoiding getting close to him even like this. Had he come out here to clear his head, too? He wasn't my business anymore, at least not on that level.

What was he really after when it came to me? Were his feelings genuine? Did it matter?

I arrived back at the palace, slipping through the window I'd left open. A chill had permeated the room, but I piled on some layers to warm me back up. Flying almost always cleared my head and brought me back to focus, but seeing Oskar out there had thrown me off. I hated this—being this off because of a male.

Even when Filip and Mylee had gotten together, I hadn't been this devastated, and I'd had feelings for Filip for much longer than I'd had feelings for Oskar. Then again, I saw how happy Filip was, happier than he'd ever been, and that made the change easier.

I blew a breath out of my nose and threw a blanket over my shoulders. Would Filip have been happy for me if I were with Oskar? Or was their rivalry too deep? Oskar thought Filip was enough of an asshole to stop me from being happy, apparently. But Filip wasn't like that. He was snarky, but all of his concern would have been for me and my emotional state, not some power trip.

I needed to talk to someone, so I called Mylee. Talking to Filip about all of this was too much, even for me. Actually, talking to anyone about my feelings overwhelmed me, but I was going stir crazy in here without an outlet. Mylee was Filip's opposite in a lot of ways—bubbly and full of life, always ready to help out a friend if they needed it.

"Hi, Daria!" Mylee said. "How are you? I'm so glad to hear from you."

Her warmth radiated through the phone, making me miss home even more intensely.

"Hey. I'm okay." I grabbed a stack of books and sat down on the couch with it, my phone cradled between my shoulder and ear. I put it on speakerphone and propped it up on the back of the couch. "How are you?"

"Not bad." Mylee paused. "Are you sure you're okay?"

I crossed my legs and put a book in my lap to scan through while we talked. Ivanna had done a spell to highlight the most pertinent information, so skimming didn't require much effort.

"Not really, actually," I said, rushing the words out before I stopped myself. "I'm just...dealing with something."

"All of the problems with the Ruler and Alphas there? Filip told me a bit about it."

"Yeah. But something else came up. Something with a guy." Filip had probably told her about his rivalry with Oskar as well, but I kept that piece of it to myself for now.

"Nothing good?" Even though we weren't on a video call, I easily imagined the way her dark brows pulled in with concern.

"Something was good. Then it wasn't." I flipped through some pages until I found the next glowing passage on seeds used as poison.

"I'm sorry, Daria."

"Thanks, but I'm the one who ended it. We have a lot of baggage, and we live so far apart," I said. "I believe what I said to him, that we'd never work out, but I still feel off about it."

"Maybe you believe it less than you thought you did. Love is scary."

Love. Gods. Was I falling in love with Oskar? I'd been in love twice, but it hadn't felt this overwhelming. That feeling had faded quickly, and we had parted ways amicably. I ran my hand along the pages of the book, even though none of the passages were glowing here.

"I agree that love is scary, but I've also been alive enough to know when I'm getting myself into more trouble than it's worth." I reached the end of the book I was holding, so I put it aside and opened the next one to skim. "But is the risk worth it?"

"What's he like? Do you see yourself with him for a long time? Putting aside the whole distance issue, I mean." I heard her open the sliding glass door at the back of their house, the crashing of the waves on the shore off in the distance.

Putting Oskar into words was difficult. All of the personality traits that had grated on me before we'd gotten close were the ones that I liked about him now: his confidence, his quick mind, his smartass smiles. Did I see myself with him in the future?

We worked well together, but being in a relationship wasn't all about work. We meshed in other ways, though. Just being with him was both comfortable and electric at the same time. He kept me on my toes, but the edgy parts of myself that I kept up for everyone else fell away.

"He's hard to explain," I finally said. "And I could see us together for the long term. But the distance is an issue, especially since I work for Filip. Plus, we have some history I won't get into."

"Hm." Mylee didn't speak for a few moments. "Let's back up. It's totally natural to grieve something like this since it was a good thing that ended. But are you sad because it's over, even though it was the right thing to do, or sad because you wish you could go back?"

I closed the book in my lap and set it aside since it didn't have much new information. "Both? I want to go way, way back to erase the past, so we wouldn't have all these obstacles. And right now, I think it was the right thing to do."

"No offense, but if you're waffling this much on whether you did the right thing, the situation might have more nuance than you thought."

She was right.

"True," I said, picking up the last book, which was on transmutation—the only original copy.

"So maybe you should talk to this guy again, whoever he is," she said. Her tone insinuated that she knew it was Oskar, but maybe I was just being paranoid. "It sounds like the way you're drawn to him overpowers the logical side of your internal argument. Obviously, going against logic isn't always the best plan, but with feelings this strong, it might be worth it."

"You're right." I opened the book to its first pages, running my hand down the old paper. "I'm going to give myself some more time to figure out exactly how I feel, but you've given me a lot to think about. Thanks, Mylee."

"Any time." The smile in her voice almost made me smile, too. "Do you know when you're coming home?"

"No, not yet." I scanned the table of contents until I found the page on rare poisons. "But I hope to come home soon. I miss everyone."

"We miss you, too," she said. "I've got to run—Audra's about to wake up from her nap."

"Okay. Give her a kiss for me."

"Will do. Bye."

We hung up. Mylee's advice was sound, but just because it made sense deep in my heart didn't mean that I was ready to walk up to Oskar and tell him that I wanted to talk about what we were yet.

I turned my attention back to the book. It was so ancient that Ivanna had done a translation spell to bring it up to somewhat modern English. If she hadn't maintained all of the spells to keep the books in good physical shape, the pages would have fallen apart in my hands.

But that boosted my confidence. All of the other books felt like rehashed versions of each other, referencing other editions in a cyclical way. Maybe something new was hiding in something this old.

I thumbed to the section on mineral poisons, something I hadn't known existed. The beginning of the section detailed how they worked. I wasn't a witch, obviously, so a lot of the more technical magic terms went over my head. But from what I gathered, certain spells could change minerals into liquid poisons that had the same effects as that mineral had in its whole form. For instance, pure iron, something that affected fae if they were cut with it, could be transformed into a liquid that could poison them from the inside out.

I turned the page, hope making my heart flutter, but when I did, a puff of air floated into my face, making my eyes sting. I coughed, rubbing at my eyes and fanning away the dust, but it sank its way into my lungs, stinging like inhaling smoke. The room lurched to the left, and my vision went completely black.

20

OSKAR

My inner circle was vast, but I didn't have as many witches and warlocks as other High Rulers. I needed more to figure out who had removed the information on ancient plants from the book I'd found, so I called in as many witches and warlocks as I could. Nearly all of the most powerful beings were here, either helping to heal Gunnar or helping to find out what someone was hiding from us.

All of them were in the library, slinging spells at the book in the hopes that it would reveal something. Another witch had already cleared Ivanna of any responsibility, so she was helping, too. I was familiar with magic, but I didn't know about the nuances of what they were doing. I just trusted them to find out what had happened.

"Have you made any progress?" I asked, walking through the library but keeping my distance from the table. Some spells bounced back, and I didn't want to be in the way.

"I think so," a warlock—who had come in from hundreds of miles away—said. "Whoever charmed the book wanted to protect it, but not necessarily hurt anyone trying to unlock it."

"So, it might not have the right information, then? It might be a red herring?" I watched a witch press her hands to the book, only for it to glow, then cough out a puff of dust.

"Possibly." The warlock grimaced.

"Keep trying. If it's a distraction, then it's a good one."

I checked my phone to see if Daria had texted to ask more questions about Gunnar, but she hadn't gotten back to me. I frowned. As much as I didn't want to think about her, I had to—she was a part of this process, so pushing her away entirely wasn't an option. But apparently, she was pushing me away.

Irritation flared up in me, both because I had to think of her when I didn't want to and because she wasn't around.

"Has anyone seen Daria?" I asked.

"I had some copies of the books we've been using made for her," Ivanna said from the far end of the long table. "I assume she's in her quarters working."

I sighed and looked to my guards near the door. "One of you fetch Daria from her quarters, please. I need her here as soon as possible."

"Yes, sir." A guard that was a bear shifter with dark hair slipped out of the room.

I watched the witches and warlocks work, my patience burning down quickly, like a wick on a stick of dynamite. Where was she? My inner circle was capable of handling this, but I needed to know where we stood regarding everything else. If this book happened to hold the secret to bringing Gunnar back from the brink, we had to start his training again immediately.

The door opened, and I expected to see Daria and the guard, but it was Freya. Her hair was up in a messy bun, as if she'd thrown it up mid-jog, and her eyes were wide. I went to her immediately, stepping outside and shutting the door.

"What's wrong?" I asked.

"The rabbit shifters," she said. "I just got a call from the captain who is overseeing the additional security for the rabbit shifters in Sweden—in Ulla's territory. The rabbit shifters and falcon shifters are fighting."

My jaw tensed. "How long has the fight been going on? Do we have enough backup to calm the conflict?"

"Not long, and they're trying to calm it down. But it's a big battle." She blew out a breath, concern in her blue eyes. "They think it's more than one pack."

I turned and walked down the hallway, her trailing behind me. If the rabbit shifters were in a physical altercation, they had probably been pushed to the far edge of their limits. They were the most peaceful shifters in my region. And if they were fighting, they were likely in their human form, where they were just as fast as they were as rabbits. But the bigger the body, the more blood could be shed.

I pushed back the memory of seeing the wolf shifters dead on the battlefield a thousand years ago, the snow stained red everywhere. As a shifter that hunted, I understood how much blood a single animal held. But seeing so much of it spread out drove the point home in an almost surreal way. I refused to see anything like that ever again. My job was to protect the beings in my region, especially against each other.

"Where are you going, sir?" Freya asked, jogging to keep up with me.

"I need to get Anja on the phone," I said. "She's been briefed, yes?"

"Of course. She's the rabbit shifter Ruler. She's the one who called me, along with the rabbit shifter Alpha of the area."

I pulled my phone from my pocket and called Anja, who picked up immediately.

"High Ruler, I've been waiting for your call," she said, annoyance laced in her voice. I allowed it, given the circumstances.

"Freya told me about the current conflict in Sweden with the falcon shifters," I said, turning the corner to go down the hall to my office. "Tell me more."

Anja sighed, a flurry of activity making the line rustle behind her. "The falcon shifters were the aggressors here, and the rabbit shifters fought back. From what the rabbit shifter Alpha has told me, it was a verbal conflict that exploded into something physical."

"Have there been any casualties?"

"Not yet, no. We have some beings from the palace who are trying to calm the situation. I'm not sure how it's going," Anja said. "This is the last thing I wanted to happen."

"I know. I agree." My guards opened the door to my office for me and Freya and closed the doors behind us once we were inside.

Someone called to Anja, and she didn't speak for several moments. She must have muted the line because it went quiet for a few beats.

"The conflict is under control, but now we have to deal with the aftermath," she said, a tinge of relief in her tone.

"I'll be there in Ruler Gunnar's stead," I said. "Expect me within the hour."

"Thank you, sir."

I hung up, turning away from Freya so she didn't see the extent of my weariness. I needed to be there—I wanted to be there, really, since I wanted the rabbit shifters to know that I supported them. But my attention was being yanked in five different directions. I took a few deep breaths to bring myself back to focus. I was more than capable of handling this, even if it was hectic. The Magic had given me more strength and stamina than nearly every other being on this planet for a reason.

"So, you're going to Ulla's territory?" Freya asked. "What about Daria?"

"Yes, I'm going. And what about Daria?" I pulled up the map of all the beings' territories and found the coordinates to Ulla's.

Freya pulled the pen that was barely holding her bun together and grabbed a hair tie from her desk. "She would be an excellent mediator in this situation."

"She would be if she were around." I looked to the guard that had followed us inside. "Have someone open a portal to take me to Ulla's territory."

The guard nodded as I told him the exact coordinates and rushed off.

"Where is she?" Freya asked.

"I don't know. The guard tasked with finding her hasn't come back yet." I grabbed my coat from the hook and slid it on. "He should have by now. Ivanna said she was probably in her quarters."

I went out into the hall again, nearly running right into the bear shifter guard I'd asked to find Daria.

"High Ruler." The guard's cheeks colored, and he bowed his head.

"Where's Daria?" I asked.

He flinched at my tone.

"I found this note on her door, sir." The guard handed me a slip of paper, which had yesterday's date across the top. It read:

I've returned home for the time being. Please contact me if you need any assistance with the matters we've been handling.

-Daria

I crumpled the note in my fist, irritation surging through my veins.

"She just left?" I asked, my voice cold and flat.

"It appears so, sir. I'm sorry."

I swore so harshly that the guard shrank back in fear. How dare she just leave like this, when I needed her? It figured. Her abilities were too good to be true, and her loyalty to Filip was stronger than her loyalty to other falcon shifters across the world. Thinking of her was a waste of my time at this point.

"I don't have time to deal with this. I can handle the situation in Ulla's territory by myself," I said. "Freya, you're in charge until I return."

"You don't want backup, sir?" she asked.

"No. I can handle this myself."

I walked to the large, empty room where witches or warlocks could open portals from one area to another. Creating one was magically intensive, so a strong warlock was already in the room, opening one up. Once it was open, I stepped through without a word. The distance from my palace to the headquarters of the rabbit shifter pack that had been attacked was short enough for one portal to take me from point A to point B.

The two rabbit shifters inside the receiving room bowed their heads in deference when I entered. They took me to the office where Anja and the Alpha of the rabbit shifter pack, Greta, were waiting. Jansen, a wolf shifter from my inner circle who I'd sent, was also at the table with them.

"High Ruler," Anja said, standing and bowing her head. "Thank you for coming on such short notice."

"This is a high priority situation, so you have my full attention." I sat down, and an attendant standing at the corner of the room approached me with a cup of tea. I accepted it, even though I didn't want it. "Tell me all of the details you have."

Anja reiterated what she had said on the phone, but I listened as if I were hearing it for the first time. She added that they'd brought the falcon shifters who were involved in the attack into custody.

"I'd like to speak with them," I said.

"You don't want to speak with the rabbits involved first?" Greta asked. "Half of the males in my pack are injured, while the falcon shifters are mostly fine."

"Since they're the aggressors, I need to talk to them to ensure that this plan isn't spreading to any other packs," I said. "Bring them here."

Anja motioned to one of the guards, who left to get the falcon shifters. She always looked slightly nervous to me—maybe it was just her instinct as a rabbit shifter near a much more powerful wolf shifter—but her expression was tense with fear today.

"I have the situation under control," I told her.

"I know." Anja pulled at a loose thread on her fluffy sweater, not meeting my eye. "It's just been a stressful couple of weeks."

Her tone didn't sit right with me, though I had no doubt that she'd had a very busy few weeks—or months, taking the conflict that some of the former Alphas had created with rabbit shifters into account.

"How are you coping?" I asked, keeping my tone gentle, even though I was on high alert inside.

"By pushing through." She looked up at me, finally. "I have to serve my rabbit shifters. The conflict with the falcon shifters has been hanging over their head long enough, and I hope we can work together to fix it."

"We will. We all will." I glanced to Jansen. He was smart, but was he picking up on the suspect tone in her voice the way I was? The subtext to her words that made me wary of her intentions? "I know that rabbits and falcons are naturally at odds, but we can work through this to find peace."

Anja nodded. "My father was Ruler before me, and he dealt with the same issues. But I'm confident that this newest crop of Alphas and the new Ruler will be just the change we need."

I locked eyes with her until she looked away, uncomfortable. The guards returned with two falcon shifters. Both were males and had superficial injuries—some bruising and cuts on their faces, and slight limps. Their hands were cuffed in front of them. Both of them looked similar enough that I assumed they were related—a little under six feet tall and lean in the powerful way falcon shifters often were.

Both averted their gazes. The guards sat them down at the far end of the table and stood behind them, close enough to unnerve them both.

"Ruler Anja tells me that you two were leading the attack against the rabbit shifters. Are you both of the same pack?" I asked.

"Yes, High Ruler," the falcon shifter with shorter, light brown hair said. The tag on his prison clothing said his name was Garth.

"And no other falcon shifter packs were involved in the fight?"

"No, sir."

I glanced at Anja and Greta. The discrepancy between what the falcon shifter was saying and what they had suggested on the phone wasn't that big of a deal, but I noted it. Maybe seeing all of the falcon shifters at once made them assume that more than one pack was involved.

"Tell me what happened and how this began." I leaned back in my seat, my posture casual. In contrast, everyone else's bodies straightened up and tensed, as I assumed they would. Seeing a High Ruler in repose was off-putting to most, which was why I did this in the first place. If the two falcons were uneasy, they were more likely to blurt out the truth whether they wanted to or not.

"Well..." The longer-haired shifter, whose name was Frederik, said, glancing at Garth. "Our hunting grounds are right alongside the rabbit's territory, as it has been for ages. But we had some rabbit shifters come into town recently to complain about falcons dipping into their land."

"It wasn't true!" Garth added. "We've been really careful since our Alpha isn't here. We don't want to start any trouble."

"And we kept telling the rabbits that—that we weren't doing anything. But they didn't believe us." Frederik shrugged, twisting his wrists within his cuffs. "And they kept threatening to tell their Ruler."

I glanced to Anja, whose face was still tight in its usual anxiety.

"We fought back. Can you blame us?" Garth shrugged, a mirror of Frederik. "They put up a fight, though. Guess it's easier to fight back with weapons in your human form than run around like a useless rabbit."

Both Anja and Greta bristled at that, so I held up a hand. They backed down.

"You're saying that the rabbit shifters instigated the attack?" I asked.

"Right. We might not like rabbit shifters, but we're not trying to start shit, like some other falcons in the territory who don't have their Alpha around." Garth scoffed. "We have better things to do."

I drummed my fingers on the table. I believed him when he said he had better things to do. This sounded like falcons retaliating so the rabbits weren't harassing them anymore. Like flicking a buzzing fly away.

"Are you aware if the rabbit shifters threatened other packs?" I asked.

"No, not that I know of," Frederik said.

"Okay." I looked to each guard. "That's all for now. We'll call you back in if we have additional questions."

The guards led the two shifters out. Once the doors shut, I sat back up.

"It seems like the rabbit shifters had more of a hand in this than you thought," I said.

Anja's face went even paler than it was. "I wasn't aware of that, sir."

"I don't blame them for being territorial. We know that the falcon shifters are in a precarious position with the Alphas gone and the Ruler still not trained," Greta added.

"I understand that, but hurling threats at falcon shifters when they claim they haven't infringed on their space feels like they wanted to start something," I said. "Interview the other rabbit shifters you have in custody to see if they corroborate the falcon's story. Since no one was killed, I feel that you two and Jansen can sort it out."

"Can you stay, High Ruler?" Anja asked, a tinge of desperation in her voice. She reached out and touched my forearm "I'd deeply appreciate your expertise in this situation. You know, considering how tense things are between rabbit and falcon shifters."

I looked down at her hand on my arm, which was an overstep. She yanked it back, lacing her fingers together on the table in front of her. I understood being overwhelmed in a tense situation, but she was the Ruler, and Greta was an Alpha. They were more than capable of handling this themselves.

Despite that, I said, "Yes, I can. For a while."

Relief washed over her features. "Thank you, sir."

"Of course."

She wasn't telling me the whole truth, but I intended to find out what it was. I had to apply more pressure, so she'd crack.

21

DARIA

I woke up with a pounding headache, a cloth over my eyes. The headache worried me less than having my strongest sense taken away from me. I panicked, jerking around and trying to get the cloth off my eyes, but my arms were bound tightly behind me. My legs were tied together at the ankle to keep me from running, but not at the knee, and my boots and socks were gone.

I stopped moving, trying to figure out where I was without injuring myself. I was on a soft surface, and when I rolled slightly to the side, I dipped inward, like I was on a couch. The sound of my struggling bounced off the walls in a way that suggested the room was huge and mostly empty. Probably tile or wood floors. My sense of smell was only slightly better than a human's, but no particularly unique scents stood out to me.

I tested the bindings around my wrists again, pulling against them to see how strong they were. The only thing I discovered was that I was weak. Maybe my headache was to blame. I groaned, rolling over onto my stomach so my face was buried in the back of the couch.

What had happened to me? I tried to ignore the constant pulsing in my temples to piece together the past. Oskar came to mind immediately, along with all of the confusion and misery surrounding him. I shoved that aside, since my love life was the least of my problems. Mylee's warm, comforting voice came next. Right—we had talked on the phone.

And I had been going over books on poisons, the one that Ivanna had given me. Dust had floated from the book to my face. It must have been charmed or enchanted to knock out whoever turned to that page.

I grimaced. I found something I shouldn't have, then. Too bad the memory of whatever it was still escaped me.

A door opened a crack, then all the way, and several sets of footsteps echoed through the room.

"She's awake," a male said. "What should we do?"

His unsure tone was unnerving. An inexperienced being was either easy to manipulate, or quick to do something stupid. I hoped it was the former.

"Help," I whispered. "Can you untie me?"

"Don't do it," a female said. "We have to keep her here."

"Please," I begged, writhing on the couch. "My head is killing me. I just need some water."

"She can't run," another male said. "She doesn't have the key."

"Fine. Get her some water," the female said.

One of them left, shutting the door behind them, and the other two came closer. Someone pulled me up so I was sitting, my feet on the floor. My bare feet touched the ice-cold ground, and I shivered.

"Did you have to take my socks off?" I asked.

"Don't answer that," the female said to the male who had stayed behind. Her voice sounded familiar, but I wasn't sure where I'd heard her before.

"So, what do we do?" the male asked.

"Nothing. We wait. Here, hold on." The female—or at least I assumed it was her from her lighter footsteps—walked away and returned moments later. I jumped when she spread a blanket over my legs, tucking it under my feet. "There. Better?"

"Yes?" Was this an elaborate prank, or were my kidnappers covering me with a blanket because I was chilly?

"We're not going to hurt you," the female said, picking up on my confusion.

"What are you intending to do? Why am I here?"

"We don't need to tell you anything," the male said. The door opened again. "We have your water, by the way."

"You didn't bring a straw?" the female asked, her tone laced with annoyance.

"We didn't have one out here."

"Fine." The female sighed. "We'll help you drink it."

Someone put the glass to my lips and tilted it back. The water was cool and crisp, so I guzzled it down.

"Thank you," I said. "Why can't you tell me what I did? Can you at least give me that? Because all I was doing was reading a book, and now I'm here."

"We can't tell you," the female said.

Again, her voice was just familiar enough to make me think. Where did I know her from? Her accent was similar to many I'd encountered in my time here—almost entirely American to the point where I would have assumed that was where they were from if I didn't know otherwise. But the non-American cadence of it was familiar. I needed to hear more from her.

"Are you in charge?" I asked. "The female."

"Sort of, yes," she said.

"Sort of?" I asked. "You aren't sure?"

"I'm sure. But a lot of us are involved..." She trailed off, as if she hadn't intended to reveal that much.

"Us meaning...?"

"I'm not telling you that, Daria," she said, her tone sharp.

Then, her identity clicked. Ivanna's assistant.

"Astrid? Is that you?" I asked. The room quieted, and I suppressed a smile. Got her. "Why did you take me?"

She rushed away, whispering for the others to follow her. The door opened and shut, leaving me alone again. At least I'd figured out part of the puzzle. Astrid was harmless, or at least she appeared to be.

What did she want with me?

I hardly knew the girl—she had helped me with my documents as much as she could without the ability to wield magic like Ivanna and brought me the books—so I had no idea who she hung out with. Were they her friends? Had Ivanna been the one to help her with the spell on the book? My heart sank at the thought. Ivanna had been Oskar's librarian witch for as long as he'd been High Ruler. Being involved in hiding what had poisoned Gunnar was a huge betrayal.

Then again, Ivanna was a witch. She had no reason to poison Gunnar or to help someone else poison him.

I sighed, wishing I had more water. At least my headache was subsiding.

I sat there, waiting for them to return, but the longer they were gone, the more ridiculous I felt for waiting. If they weren't going to hurt me, I had no reason to comply. I leaned over, rubbing my face on the couch to push the covering over my eyes up. They'd tied it tightly, and I was too weak to go quickly, but with some work, I got the eye covering off.

I squinted against the light of the room, even though it was low. As I suspected, it was mostly empty, like a storage space for unwanted furniture. Some broken wooden chairs were to my left, and a scratched-up armchair was to my right. Folded up tables were propped up against the wall near the door.

I straightened my legs to see what kind of restraints were around my ankles. Charmed ropes, which explained why I was so weak. The faint glow intensified the more I moved.

I scanned the room for possible ways to get the ropes off or get to someone for help. My vision was strong enough to see every single crack in the wall, even at a distance. Aside from the door, which I assumed was locked, no exits were available. I rubbed against my ropes again, the energy draining from my limbs.

But I had to push past it. The broken chairs had sharp edges for me to rub the ropes against. The ropes were charmed to sap my energy and to stop me from shifting, but some were able to be cut.

The door swung open again before I tried to get over there. It was Astrid, though I didn't recognize the two males. Based on their slight, wiry frames, they were also rabbit shifters. Astrid's eyes widened when she noticed I'd gotten my eye covering off. She slammed the door closed and sighed.

"We should have tied it tighter," one of the males said.

"Does it matter?" the other, the smallest of the three, asked. "She guessed who Astrid was."

"Quiet, both of you," Astrid hissed, approaching me.

"Astrid, can't you tell me why you brought me here? You had something to do with the book, didn't you?" I asked, softening my voice and looking up at her, as if I weren't able to tear out their throats in an instant in my falcon form. "Was that why you were so nervous when you dropped it off?"

Astrid paced back and forth, her arms crossed over her chest. "You weren't supposed to have it."

"So why didn't you take it back?" I asked.

"Because that might have been more suspicious?" Astrid pressed the heels of her hands to her forehead. "I don't know. I'm so stupid. I was just intimidated and made the wrong decision."

"Astrid..." The taller male put his hand on her shoulder. "We shouldn't."

"It doesn't really matter, does it?" Astrid asked, her eyes watery. "We're erasing her memory, anyway."

"Erasing my memory? Hold on." I held myself still so I wouldn't drain my energy against the charmed ropes. "Explain."

"The serum hasn't gotten here yet," the shorter male said in a low voice.

"But it's definitely on the way. They said it would be another few hours, but they're in transit." Astrid stopped in front of me, her hands on her hips. "She'll forget it all."

My heart pounded, but I maintained my calm energy. "Forget what?"

"We're not trying to hurt anyone," she reiterated. "We're just trying to protect ourselves."

I nodded for her to continue. "From what?"

"From falcon shifters," the shorter male said. "You've always targeted us because we aren't the strongest out there, but being weaker doesn't mean we shouldn't exist. The falcon shifters have always wanted to take over. Luckily, High Ruler Oskar thwarted the plot the falcon shifter Alphas had to massacre us."

"It gave us the perfect opportunity, too. We figured we could destabilize them with their leadership in disarray," Astrid said, sitting cross-legged on the ground a few feet from me. "If we seeded a little discord between the Alphas to get them to fight against each other and not us, we'd be safer. And if we killed Ruler Gunnar, we'd have even more time to build up our numbers and make more alliances to protect ourselves."

"What do you mean by seeding discord between the Alphas?" I asked, frowning.

"Just getting them to fight over power and petty matters like rumors." Astrid waved her hand.

"Like the one about Artem flirting with Klaus' mate," I said, the memory making much more sense.

"Exactly," the short male said. "It's working, isn't it?"

"So, you thought by killing the falcon shifter Ruler, you could gain more power?" I asked, ignoring the short male's question. "Even though the Magic would choose another in the event of Gunnar's death?"

"Eventually. We've made some protection alliances with the witches and warlocks." Astrid shrugged.

"We meaning who?"

"We shouldn't say more," the taller male said, his eyes darting between me and Astrid. "What if the serum doesn't get here?"

Astrid bit her bottom lip, tugging absently at her ponytail. "You're right. I should stop."

"Shut up, then." The taller male jerked his head toward the door. "Cover her eyes again."

"Who are you working with?" I asked again, dropping the sweet act.

"Come *on*," the taller male said, walking out.

Astrid got to her feet and followed, as did the shorter male. Shit.

"Do the right thing, Astrid!" I called after her.

She threw me one more look over her shoulder, her face bone white, before shutting the door behind her.

I sank back into the couch cushions, my heart sinking. At least I'd gotten some information. But what was I supposed to do with it while locked away and tied up? I believed Astrid when she said they weren't going to hurt me, but I didn't want them to wipe my memory with this serum they'd said they had.

I closed my eyes, my body weak and exhausted. I had to figure out how to tell Oskar before it was too late.

22

OSKAR

Anja was doing a damn good job at stalling. She'd dragged me around to various meetings and interrogations. My presence helped in all of them, but I wasn't absolutely necessary. Anja and Greta were capable of handling this themselves.

"I need to go," I said after we left another rabbit shifter's interrogation room. The shifter had the same story as the others—that the falcon shifters were threatening them by hunting in their area. "I have business to attend to, and you both have this covered."

"Are you sure, High Ruler?" Anja asked, checking her phone before clutching it in both hands.

"I'm extremely sure. I've heard enough." I stepped into her space. I was well over a foot and a half taller than her, but even if we were the same height, I'd overpower her. I rarely used my size like this, but my patience was wearing thin. "What's the real reason I'm here, Anja? Because you're stalling."

Anja took a step back. "We're just...overwhelmed. We aren't stalling. I'm telling the truth."

I studied her face, even as she looked everywhere but at me. I swept my gaze to Greta, whose eyes were pinned to the ground.

"Look at me, Anja. I've been way too generous with you already, but I'm giving you one more chance to tell me the truth. The full truth," I said, making her visibly shudder in fear. "Give me the real reason why you're asking me to stay."

My phone rang, and both Greta and Anja relaxed. It was Filip. Of course he'd call at the least convenient time. I sent it to voicemail right away. I wasn't interested in what he had to say. But he called back immediately.

"Yes?" I barked, stepping away from the rabbit shifters.

"You're seriously going to send my call to voicemail?" Filip asked with a condescending tone that grated on my nerves.

"What did you need, Filip?"

"Daria's not answering my calls. Where did you put her?" he asked.

"Where did I put her?" I scoffed, walking further down the hall. "Does she know you talk about her like she's a piece of furniture?"

"You're sidestepping the point," Filip growled. "Daria always answers my calls. Where is she?"

His words finally sank in. "I got a note that she was going home yesterday. Is she not there?"

"No. How would she have gotten home? Portal? Plane?"

"Plane, I'm assuming. I have private ones with pilots available at any hour of the day." Panic started to climb up my throat. "So, she's not there?"

"Would I bother calling you if she were?" he shot back, though the anxiety in his voice was noticeable.

"Shit." I breezed past Anja and Greta, temporarily muting the call to talk to my guards. "Get the portal back to my palace ready."

"Why would she say she was leaving?" Filip asked. "Are you done?"

I unmuted the call. "No, we…had a disagreement. She was upset. Her note said that she was going home."

"What did you say to her?!" he shouted.

"Not the point. The point is that Daria left a note saying she was leaving to go home, and she isn't there. And I'm away from my palace, so I don't know if anyone else has seen her lately." I pushed past several members of the Alpha's staff and back into the room where my portal had opened. Two warlocks were still working on it. "How much longer until the portal is open?"

"Any second, sir."

"Find Daria and keep me updated." Filip hung up right as the portal opened.

I rushed through the portal, my guards close behind, and out of the portal room. I called Freya right away.

"Freya, have you seen Daria?" I asked.

"No. I thought she went home?"

"Has *anyone* seen her since she said she left?" I broke into a run, outpacing my security with ease.

"I don't know. I'll ask around. I'm in the library right now," Freya said.

"Good, call me back as soon as you know. And look up the flight logs to see if she took one of the planes. I shouldn't have assumed that she did without checking."

I hung up and burst outside, crossing the palace grounds toward the guest quarters. My guard had said she'd left a note on the door, but he hadn't checked inside. I reached the doors to her quarters and yanked the door open, pulling it clear off its hinges.

"Daria?" I called. "Daria?"

I looked in her office, which looked like someone had hastily thrown things around in search of something—probably a book, if the ones on the floor were any indication. Her laptop charger was still there, which she wouldn't have forgotten. Panic nearly blinded me as I checked the bathroom, then her bedroom. The lights were off, so I flipped them on. The rooms were also turned upside down. I ripped open her closet and checked under her bed for her suitcase, but it was gone too.

Someone had taken her.

A barrage of regrets flew through my head. I shouldn't have let her walk around without a guard, even though she had insisted she was fine. And I shouldn't have pushed her away after our argument.

We worked well together and could have despite our romantic relationship not working out.

Freya called me back, frantic.

"No, no one's seen her, and no one took any flights out," she said. "I'm getting the security footage right now."

I dug my hand into my hair and pulled, panic threatening to close my windpipe. "Meet me in my office to go over it."

I looked around her office again, since she had spent so much time in there. It was as if she'd been plucked right from her desk in the middle of working.

I shoved past my guards, fear like I'd never known spurring me back to my office. Maybe she had left and flown home? It was an astronomically huge stretch, but I needed some form of hope to hold onto.

I burst into my office, finding Freya and my head of security, Tim, at her computer.

"High Ruler, we found some footage," Tim said, stepping back so I could see the screen.

Two forms, a male and a female, appeared at the end of the hallway, rushing toward Daria's room with their heads bowed toward each other. We didn't have audio, but the frantic way they moved their hands gave away their anxiety. Even through the screen, I sensed that the female was a rabbit shifter, and the male was a warlock.

The female looked up just long enough for me to recognize her. Astrid?

"Astrid was there earlier," Freya said. "She delivered books to Daria."

I kept my eyes on the security footage. The warlock, who had kept his face hidden, opened the door. I sped through the security footage until the door opened again. Daria wasn't with them, but her big suitcase was. I assumed she was inside, since unauthorized cloaking magic would have tipped off the spells around my palace. The bag was so nondescript that no one would have given the warlock a second look for dragging it around, since he had security clearance at my headquarters.

Astrid disappeared out of frame for a second before reappearing, sticking a note to the door and writing on it as she referenced her phone. Then, she left again.

Tim flipped through the security feeds, following them as they pulled Daria's suitcase through the palace grounds. My stomach twisted in knots. Their plan was far from genius, but it was simple enough to work. They loaded the suitcase with Daria in it into the back of a car and left.

Was she alive in there? Or had someone hurt her?

"Find a witch or warlock to analyze her room and see if any spells were done, particularly if they're harmful."

"Of course, sir." Tim made a phone call and confirmed that someone was on their way to check out her room.

I sank down into my desk chair. I didn't want to feel powerless when it came to Daria. Our argument disappeared from my memory, and only the good moments played in my head. I missed her, and if I never got to see her again after leaving on such a negative note, I'd never forgive myself.

Freya and I waited for news on what had happened in Daria's room, the silence thick in the air. Finally, Tim got a call.

"Magic was used, but it was a spell—something to knock her out and not kill her," he said after he ended the call.

My shoulders sagged in relief. "The odds are good that she's alive?"

"Assuming we find her, yes. The odds are pretty good," Tim said. "I've put a search out for the car that was in the security footage."

"Which direction did they go?" I asked, standing up.

"Northwest."

"They're probably going to abandon the car. The roads out that way aren't good," I said. "We need to get a search party on the ground. Gather as many members of my inner circle as you can, and all of the security except the most necessary members."

"Yes, sir."

Even if no one was available to search, I would have gone out by myself and torn the country apart trying to find her.

If anyone hurt her...

A lightning bolt of emotion raced through me so quickly that I had to put my hand on the wall to steady myself. All of the feelings I had for Daria intensified by several orders of magnitude, taking it beyond affection and even love.

Mine.

Daria was mine. My wolf claimed her, my primal senses finally acknowledging the intensity of my feelings for her.

She became everything for me—my mate. Daria, of all females. But she made more sense to me in that moment than anything or anyone else had in my entire existence.

The idea of letting her go was unfathomable, like splitting myself in half. I had to find her.

I went outside and shifted, raising my nose high to possibly catch her scent in the wind. I ran off to the northwest, my legs moving as fast as they could.

23

DARIA

The wait for Astrid and the two other shifters to return with their serum was agonizing. Having my memories erased sounded so invasive, even if they weren't going to kill me or even hurt me. How many memories were they going to take? Memory wiping serums were made with dark, illegal magic, so I had no idea how it was going to work. What if they erased all of my memories? What if I forgot who I was?

I'd forget Oskar, too, or at least what we'd had while I was here. But at least I'd forget the pain along with that.

I squeezed my eyes shut, gathering my strength.

I rolled off the couch, landing with a thump, and inched my way toward the broken chairs. The distance felt so much longer now that I was trying to get there with these charmed ropes around my wrists and ankles.

I froze at the sound of footsteps in the hallway. A few people had passed by the door, but none had stopped in front of it or come in. Was this a huge house? The size of it reminded me of a school's basement. Then again, I had no idea how long I'd been out, so I might have been in an entirely different country. If I got these ropes off and managed to fight my way out of here, I'd fly as long as it took to get to safety.

The footsteps continued down the hall, but more came back. I curled up into a ball and leaned against the couch when the door opened again. It was Astrid, holding a plate of food; some bread, smoked fish, and potatoes from the smell of it. My stomach growled.

"I brought you food," Astrid said. "Why are you on the floor?"

"I rolled too far and fell," I said since that technically wasn't a lie. "Thank you."

She came over to me with the tray and sat on the couch. "I can't untie you, sorry. I hope it's not awkward that I'm feeding you."

"It's fine." It was more awkward that she was being so nice when she'd played a part in taking me hostage. "It's not... The serum isn't in the food, is it?"

"No." She cut off a piece of the bread, spread a bit of butter on it, and added the fish before taking a bite. "See?"

"Thank you."

She pulled me back up onto the couch, then buttered some bread for me. Taking one bite made me groan embarrassingly loud.

"Isn't it good?" she said. "The bread is my favorite."

I chewed and swallowed, nodding. She kept feeding me bites, adding some of the fish to the bread, too. I wasn't sure about the combination at first, but it was surprisingly good. She ate a potato to show me that they weren't laced with the serum, then fed me those as well.

"Astrid, can you tell me who created this plan? It wasn't you, was it?" I asked.

"I really can't say."

"But you're going to wipe my memory. Does it really matter?" I made myself smaller by hunching a little bit, hoping she'd take pity on me. She was way too soft to be in the kidnapping business.

Astrid sighed, eating another potato almost absently.

"It doesn't, but I still shouldn't." She fed me another potato.

"Can you tell me about the witches and warlocks you've been making alliances with? Is Ivanna one of them?"

Astrid took her time buttering more bread. "Ivanna isn't. She has nothing to do with this. They agreed to help us because one of our Alphas is married to the warlock Ruler. He'd do anything to help her and the rabbit shifters."

I waited for her to say more, but she didn't. I had to change up my strategy, then. She was a softie, but someone had gotten to her to keep her from talking to me more. What would push a nice female like Astrid into taking part in a kidnapping? Protecting herself from falcon shifters, yes, but wasn't that what most rabbit shifters wanted? Something had pushed her to the edge.

"How do you know those other two rabbit shifters who were with you?" I asked. "Are they your friends?"

She nodded. "Yeah. Same pack."

"You've known them your whole life? You're close?"

"Pretty much. We were neighbors when we were younger." Astrid held up the fork, another potato on its tines, and I opened my mouth for it. I chewed the potato, letting the conversation dip, so she didn't feel like I was interrogating her.

"How has your pack been doing? A lot of conflicts have been popping up lately," I said. "With the falcon shifters, I mean."

Astrid's eyes darkened. At first, I thought she was angry, but she was upset.

"Not good. We've had some losses," she said. "And some injuries. We've been dealing with falcon shifters for centuries. Or at least that's what my family says. I'm only thirty, so I am just going by what they tell me."

"I'm sorry to hear that," I said.

"You're a falcon, though. Why do you care?" she asked, not unkindly. "I thought all of you hated rabbit shifters. Aren't regular rabbits your prey?"

"We don't. Or at least I don't," I said. "We don't have many rabbit shifters in my region, but my High Ruler is a strong advocate of keeping the peace. And all of the Rulers under him have come to agree."

Astrid laughed humorlessly, pushing the last few pieces of potato around on the plate. "How does he do it? How does he get everyone to agree?"

"He doesn't. People just fall in line when they follow his leadership." I shrugged. "He's one of the original magical beings, though, so he commands a lot of respect."

Astrid put the fork down, her shoulders slumped. "I don't know if anything will ever change. I know High Ruler Oskar is doing everything he can to help—I can see that from the inside—but it all feels so helpless."

"Is that why you're going through with this plan to kill Ruler Gunnar? Because it's the only way you feel like you can make a change?" My voice was barely above a whisper, even though my blood was rushing through my veins. I was so close to getting her to crack.

"Yeah. All of us are on board with it, even though we don't like violence. We've reached the end of our ropes. The whole region is involved at this point." Astrid's eyes cut toward the door before she looked back to me. "I shouldn't have said anything."

"You're erasing my memory, so I won't know." I looked at the door as well, my stomach churning. I had the info, but I had no way to get out. "How much longer will I be here?"

"I don't know." Astrid got up. "I just know they told me to feed you because it makes the serum work better. I have to go. I'm sorry for doing this. I know it won't hurt, at least."

I bit the inside of my cheek so hard that I tasted blood. I needed a damn plan and fast.

I leaned over to see what was in the hallway when Astrid left. I only saw the other side of the hall, which was a white-painted concrete wall. Someone was walking in the hallway, but the doors closed before I saw who it was.

I pulled against my ropes, groaning at the strain it put on my body. If they were going to use the serum on me soon, I didn't have time to cut the ropes using the edge of one of the broken chairs. My only hope was if they untied me when they gave me the serum... which was unlikely.

I took a slow, steady breath. I was going to figure this out.

I waited until the door opened again to formulate a solid plan. Astrid, the shorter rabbit shifter who had been with her before, and a male I didn't recognize came in. The male had a vial in his hands—the memory erasing serum, I assumed. His skin was deathly pale, like he was sick and not just fair.

The two rabbit shifters looked at the unknown male, the only one of the three who appeared sure of himself. I swallowed the lump in my throat as they approached. Rabbit shifters were incredibly fast, both in their human forms and rabbit forms, so outrunning them wasn't an option. I had to push myself and fight back despite the magic ropes draining my energy. My options were limited. I'd fight until I passed out.

"Hold her still," the male I didn't know said.

Astrid and the short male rabbit shifter were by my side in an instant, each one holding an arm. I struggled against their grips. The only thing stopping me from beating them both were the ropes pulling away every ounce of strength I had.

The male grabbed my face, his grip tight.

I squirmed, even as the edges of my vision darkened. The male held the vial up to my lips, trying to force my mouth open, but I jerked my head back, sending the vial to the ground. My heart leapt in my chest, hoping I'd given myself enough time.

The male swore, picking it back up before it spilled all the way.

"Is it still going to work?" the short male rabbit shifter asked, still holding onto me.

"Should work. It won't be as foolproof, though." The unknown male lifted the vial and shrugged, reaching for me again. All of the energy and fight had gone out of me, but he grabbed me by the throat anyway.

I squeezed my eyes closed as he pushed the vial against my lips. As hard as I tried, the cold, bitter liquid slid into my mouth. The flavor made me retch, but the male held me still. And I held it in my mouth, my eyes watering. Was it going to absorb this way? I wasn't sure. But like hell was I swallowing it.

"Make her swallow," Astrid said, still gripping my arm.

A commotion broke out beyond the door, loud enough for all of us to hear it. The male let go of my neck and ran toward the door, giving me the chance to spit it out. My head spun, my thoughts turning sluggish. It was too late. Some must have gotten down my throat.

I slumped against the seats, the scene hazy in front of me. The room took on a dreamlike quality, like I was observing from afar. All of the chaos and sound in the hallway was equally distant, yet close at the same time. Astrid and the short male rabbit shifter leapt from the couch, leaving me there. My body slumped to the side without their support, and I laid on the couch, feeling glued to the surface.

My eyelids were heavy, but I kept them open just in time to see several shifters burst through the door—foxes, bears, and wolves.

One big, white wolf stood out in particular: Oskar.

Seeing him in his wolf form cleared my mind so abruptly that I gasped. He was the flash of light across a dark sky, brightening every-thing around me, filling me with hope and happiness and love like I'd never known before. His presence filled a space in my soul that I hadn't realized was empty, a space made just for him.

The feeling was so intense that I knew I wasn't dreaming—it was real. My entire reality shifted into a new place as the realization clicked. Oskar was my mate. No one else would ever replace him or connect with me on the level that we'd been joined. The permanence of the bond didn't scare me at all—it felt natural, like it had always been there. My future wasn't mapped out, but I knew he was going to be in it, and that was enough for me.

He shifted back into his human form in front of me and kneeled, running his trembling hands over my face and arms, checking for injuries.

"Daria, can you hear me? Are you all right?" he asked, his tone so nakedly afraid that it hurt my heart. Was I feeling his emotions through our mate bond? The sensation was so surreal.

The fog in my thoughts came back, robbing me of my ability to speak. I groaned instead.

"I've got you," Oskar said, tearing the ropes off my wrists and ankles with ease.

Every cell in my body relaxed, as if the magic in the bonds had been squeezing everything dry for as long as they'd been on. I threw my arms around him, sobbing into his chest. He swept his big hand up and down my back, pulling our bodies close enough together to feel each other's heartbeats. The pounding of his against mine comforted me in ways I didn't know were possible.

"You're safe," he murmured, his heart slowing down. "You're safe."

"You came," I choked out, holding onto him even tighter. The room still spun, so he held me up, steadying me physically and emotionally.

"I had to the moment I learned you'd been taken," he said, pulling back. "Nothing was going to stop me from getting to you."

I started crying all over again.

"But our argument...and—"

He put a finger to my lips. "It's in the past, Daria. Focus on what we have now because it feels so damn good."

And it did. I'd never been so relieved or so elated or so exhausted in my life, much less all of those feelings at the same time.

Locking eyes with him brought me to another high, so intense that it nearly took my breath away. I kissed him, giving him everything I had. But I didn't have much left. My vision browned out at the edges until I passed out. The last thing I remembered was him catching me.

24

OSKAR

Daria slumped into my arms. The panic that had spurred me on during my search came back until I realized that she was still breathing—she had just fainted. Now that she was still, I checked her for injuries again. Aside from some abrasions where the ropes had rubbed against her skin, which were rapidly healing, she was fine. But had she been poisoned, too?

I picked up the vial near her feet, lifting it to my nose. Most of it had spilled on the ground, but she might have ingested some. The idea of Daria ending up like Gunnar, stuck in a coma while I stood by helplessly, brought me to the lowest low. If the thought of it were this devastating, I never wanted to know what life would feel like without her. I wasn't sure I'd survive.

"Sir, we've secured the area," one of my guards said from behind me.

"Good. Bring me a witch or warlock. I need someone to tell me what this is as soon as possible," I said, holding up the vial.

"Yes, sir."

I pulled Daria into my lap, holding her close. Her skin was chilled, as I suspected it often was here, and she looked surprisingly peaceful. The two-way flow of our emotions was muted by her being passed out, but she wasn't in pain from what I could tell. Good. I never wanted her to hurt. It was worse than being in pain myself.

I brought her closer, kissing her forehead. With the help of the security footage and me catching Daria's scent, we'd found the building where they'd taken her. It was an old research station that humans had long abandoned. Fighting inside hadn't been hard—most of the beings there were rabbit shifters, with some witches and warlocks acting as defense.

I'd burst past all of them, my guards and backup covering me. The need to protect Daria was so intense that I would have fought every last one of them if they had stood in my way.

Moments later, a witch arrived. I handed her the vial, and she checked what it was with a spell.

"It's not lethal, is it?" I asked, looking up at the witch. I didn't want to move Daria any more than I already had.

"No, it's not. It's a memory erasing serum," the witch said.

"A memory erasing serum?" I took the vial back. "How much of her memory has been erased? Most of it spilled, from what I can tell."

"It's hard to know for sure. It takes some time to work. The magic is probably working through her faster now that she's passed out." The witch squatted down next to us. "Let me see what I can do."

I shifted Daria on my lap, so she was sitting up. The witch put a hand on Daria's forehead, closing her eyes in concentration. Daria stirred, groaning softly, but the witch didn't stop what she was doing. Eventually, Daria went still again, her lips slightly parted. Now she looked asleep rather than unconscious.

"I did a spell to slow down the magic of the serum for now. We'll need to get her back to a healer who can undo the effects of it. We'll have to see the extent of her memory loss when she wakes up."

I ran my fingers through Daria's soft hair. "Do you think she'll remember me?"

"I'm sure she will. If she only drank a small amount, I doubt the damage is extensive." The witch smiled, standing up. "But we should get back to get her the help she needs."

I got up, keeping Daria in my arms, and went outside. The fight hadn't been bloody, to my relief, and my inner circle were making arrests. With so many of them to process and interview, we'd have our hands full again. All I knew was that the rabbit shifters were involved, and my gut told me that Anja knew about this.

I kept Daria in my arms the entire drive home, not even letting her go when we got up to the healers' room. Eventually, they had me put her on a cot, but I stayed next to her.

A healer witch made Daria more comfortable, working spells to wake her up out of her slumber and reverse the effects of the serum. It took longer than I wanted it to, but seeing Daria's eyes open and clear was worth the wait.

"Oskar? Where am I?" she asked, her voice hoarse.

"You're in the healers' room," I said, cupping her cheek. "How do you feel?"

"Strange. But not in an entirely bad way." She rested her hand on top of mine. "I was about to say that being your mate is what's throwing me off, but it feels so right."

"It feels right to me, too." Against the odds. I kissed her forehead, then her temple, then her lips.

Our previous kiss had felt desperate, like she was trying to convey her feelings to me as quickly as possible before she passed out. But this was lazy, the kind of kiss we could sink into and enjoy every moment of now that we were safe. And we did, not minding the sound beyond the curtain. A healer made a small sound of surprise near the opening and left, reminding me that we still had so much to cover.

"We were getting carried away there. We can pick up on that later," I said, brushing my thumb along her bottom lip.

"Okay." Daria's near-shyness was painfully endearing. "When I get my head on straight, I mean. It's all kind of hazy."

"In what way?"

"Like I know memories are there, but a cloud is covering them. Bits and pieces of full memories are there, though."

"Do you remember anything specific?" I asked.

Daria frowned, leaning against me. "I'm trying to."

My heart sank. "What's the last thing you remember?"

She sat up, momentarily putting space between us before tucking herself against my side again. I put my arm around her more securely.

"I remember calling home when I was in my quarters. Then I remember passing out after opening a book," she said. "The book was what drugged me—it was a book on transmutation."

"The book drugged you? What do you mean?"

"I mean, I opened the page, and some dust blew up in my face."

My blood ran cold, and I pulled her closer, almost on instinct. "Like someone was trying to stop you from seeing the information that was there."

"Exactly." She squeezed the bridge of her nose, like her head hurt. "I feel like there's something else about it that I need to remember, but it's not coming to me."

"Just breathe, okay? You don't have to have all the answers right now. The spells to reverse the serum take time." I kissed her softly, then again, and her pleasure washed over me. "Do you think the book is still in your room?"

"It might be. I remember that it was old while the others I had were duplicates that Ivanna made." Remembering something lifted her spirits.

"Good." I got the attention of one of my guards. "Bring us the books that are in Daria's quarters. Don't open them. They might be enchanted."

"Right away, sir."

The guard left, giving us more space. All of the other guards were posted outside of the room, and healers were still tending to Gunnar one room over. I hoped the books had the answer to whatever had poisoned him.

"How are you feeling?" I asked, pushing my fingers through her hair. Touching her soothed parts of me I never knew existed until today. All I wanted to do was make sure the world was better for her to be in.

"Fine. But stupid." Daria leaned into my touch.

"It's not your fault that the serum—"

"Not because of the serum. Because of pushing you away before because of our past," Daria said. A tinge of insecurity came through our bond, and I frowned. "It was my fear talking. And my insecurities. I'm sorry."

"Forget about the past. We both made mistakes. Now that we're mates, we have eternity to create a better future. You don't need to feel insecure about anything."

She was still curious about something. I wasn't sure if it was because of us, or just because she'd lost her memory.

"Can I ask you about Freya?" She looked up at me, a worried wrinkle between her brows. I smoothed it with my thumb.

"What about her?"

"You two aren't..." She gestured vaguely, but I got her message.

"Of course not." I held back the urge to snort since she was genuinely worried about this.

"Freya's just my second-in-command and close friend. Nothing more."

Her energy calmed down significantly, maybe because she felt my sincerity.

"You'll have to get along with Filip. Or at least be cordial," she said, a hint of warning in her tone.

The stirring of feelings flowing through our mate bond gave me pause. She was still worried about this, even though the mate bond was the most unbreakable, intense bond in existence.

"We will. We'll talk it out." The idea of doing it made me vaguely queasy, but the pleasure that she felt knowing I'd try eased my nerves. "I'd do anything for you, Daria."

She looked up at me, a smile in her brown eyes. "I love you."

"I love you, too." I lifted her chin and kissed her.

The kiss deepened fast, our bodies tangling together on the tiny bed. Feeling her arousal through our bond made my cock so hard that it ached in a matter of moments. But we were still in the healers' room—the first time we made love as mates wasn't going to be on a bed that hardly fit both of us on it. I broke the kiss, settling her back down on the pillows.

"It's weird feeling this happy in the middle of all this turmoil," she said. "I hope my memories come back so I can help."

"I think you've already helped by remembering the book that made you pass out. We already found a book that had some information removed from it. I'm guessing this one was altered for similar reasons."

Someone cleared their throat outside the curtain, and I told them to come in. It was Ivanna.

"I have the books, sir, both the ones from Daria's room and the one that had the information removed from it," she said. Her eyes were rimmed with dark circles, and I didn't blame her. "And I've analyzed them with spells. This old one had a knock-out spell in it, but I've neutralized it."

I extended my hand, and she put the old book in it.

"Do you remember where the page was?" I asked Daria, putting the book between us.

"I think so." She opened the book to the table of contents, then found the page she was looking for. She flipped through until she found what she needed. "This. This is it."

I scanned the page, chills running down my spine. It described how to transmute the mineral Pator into a liquid form. Pator was incredibly rare and was one of the few minerals that was able to seriously hurt—and even kill—powerful shifters in a large enough quantity. It weakened them significantly to the point where their shifter abilities were rendered useless.

Usually, it was forged into weapons, but apparently, a witch or warlock could change it into liquid form if they got their hands on enough of it. How whoever had poisoned Gunnar had gotten it was beyond me—it was rare to the point where most healers didn't think of it when dealing with illnesses.

"Pator?" Daria's eyes widened. "Wouldn't it have a flavor if it was a rock? Or would transmuting it change the flavor?"

I skimmed the paragraph for more information.

"It has a salty flavor, which I guess could be hidden if you tried hard enough.

Let me see the other book," I said. Daria handed it to me, and I turned to the marked page. "*Making flavorless potions with herbs.* I guess they wanted to be careful to make sure he didn't say anything about any strange tasting food."

"Is there anything on the antidote?" Daria asked, frantically turning through the old book.

"It doesn't matter. We can have someone find it." I slid off the bed and pushed back the curtain, where the healers were working. "Ruler Gunnar was poisoned with Pator. I need as many of you as possible to find the solution."

The healers flew into action right away.

I looked back at Daria, who eased herself out of bed.

"Should we get out of their way?" she asked.

"Are you okay to walk?" I rushed to her side, putting my arm around her. She looked up at me, raising an eyebrow. I snorted at the annoyance rippling through her. "Sorry."

"That's handy." She grinned. "I don't even have to sass you anymore. I can just feel it in your direction."

"I have the feeling that you're going to sass me anyway." I threaded my fingers in hers. "Come on. We have some work to do, if you're up to it."

"I don't think I can rest until we get this sorted out."

We left, heading back to my office. Freya was inside, her fingers on her temple as if she had a headache. When we walked in, she brightened.

"Daria! You're already up? You're okay?" She stood, rushing over to us.

"Yeah, I'm fine. A healer witch did some spells to start reversing the effects of the memory erasing serum." Daria adjusted her hair.

"Memory erasing serum?" Freya looked between us both. "And... you're mates?"

"Yeah." I smiled. Everyone could sense a mate bond—it was that powerful. "It's been a busy day."

"That's an understatement. Congratulations. Sit, sit." Freya waved Daria over to the couch. "I'm sure you've already been asked about what's happened, Daria. We have a ton of rabbit shifters, witches, and warlocks in custody at the moment, and we're working through interviewing them."

"Astrid told me everything. More or less," Daria said. "The rabbit shifters poisoned Gunnar to weaken the falcon shifters and tried to turn them against each other."

"How did you get her to confess?" I asked.

"She thought they were going to erase my memory for good." Daria shrugged. "And she was guilty, I think. She never wanted to hurt me. She even fed me, though that was to make the serum work better. All she wanted was to keep rabbit shifters safe. Not that it excuses poisoning anyone or causing any harm, but I understand her in some ways."

Her empathy for the shifters who had kidnapped her and planned to wipe her memory of it astonished me. Even if they hadn't hurt her, they had planned to violate her thoughts.

"Was Astrid the mastermind of the whole plan?" I asked.

Daria frowned again. "I don't know. I guess more of my memory will come back."

"I doubt Astrid is the mastermind of anything, no offense to her," Freya said. "She's very soft-spoken and sweet."

"She was a part of a plot to kill a Ruler, so her kindness won't save her," I said. "We should go talk to her since she's been so willing to open up."

Daria's spirit sank. I reached over and squeezed her leg.

"I don't have a choice," I murmured to her.

"I know. It doesn't make it any easier." Daria straightened up. "Let's go talk to her and get some answers."

The prisoners' quarters were a few miles away, at the edge of my palace grounds, so one of my drivers took all three of us there. The guards at the front took us straight to Astrid, who was curled up on a bench in a cell toward the back of the building. She glanced up at us when we appeared in the doorway, bowing her head more out of shame than deference.

"High Ruler," Astrid said, her voice wobbling.

"We have some questions for you, Astrid." I waited for the guards to put some seats inside for the three of us before pulling out a seat for Daria.

"Of course. I will tell you whatever you need to know."

I sat next to Daria, lifting an eyebrow. "Most criminals aren't willing to spill all of their secrets."

"I'm not a criminal." Astrid sat up, looking between me and Daria. "I've just...done some crimes."

Freya managed to quiet her snort before it came out.

"Daria says you told her about the reasons why you kidnapped her—to stop her from finding out about what poisoned Ruler Gunnar," I said. Astrid nodded. "But who's at the top of all of this?"

"Ruler Anja." Astrid curled back up, her knees to her chest.

My suspicions were right, then, and the entire plot made sense. Instead of razing the falcons with violence the way they had been attacked, they had tried to destabilize them. Poisoning Gunnar was still an assassination attempt, but of all the conflicts between shifters that I'd dealt with, this was one of the tamer ones.

"Where did she get the Pator that poisoned Ruler Gunnar?" Daria asked.

"The warlock Ruler, I think." Astrid rubbed at her eyes, even though she wasn't crying. At least not yet. "They were going to protect us—an alliance. I'm not sure where the warlock got it, though, but he processed it. I brought him the book on the transmutation process, and he put the spell on it. I tried to keep it deep in the stacks so Ivanna wouldn't find it, but she did."

Astrid sniffed, crying quietly. "What's going to happen to us?" she asked. "For being a part of this."

"We'll need to gather more information from the others before we decide. And talk to Ruler Anja, of course. Thank you for speaking with us." I blew out a sigh. I didn't want to have to put more leaders to death, but Anja's crimes, assuming Astrid was telling the truth, were serious. Being High Ruler required empathy, but not being too soft.

We left, gathering in the entryway.

"I don't want to tell you how to do your job, but I think she deserves a lighter sentence. Not just her—all of the rabbit shifters that were involved but didn't hurt anyone, too," Daria said.

I ran a hand through my hair. "I'll consider it. I don't want anyone believing that they can do things like this and get away with it."

Daria looked in the direction of Astrid's cell, her emotions stirring. I wanted her to be happy, but I wanted to be just. She turned her attention back to me, sensing my dilemma. She squeezed my hand, the simple gesture reassuring me that she trusted my judgment.

After all of the conflict we'd had, it was meaningful. We'd gotten over the worst of the mess we'd been handed, but we still had more to tackle. Knowing she was by my side made it easier to bear.

25

DARIA

The side effects of the memory erasing serum and the spells that had been used to undo it lingered the rest of the day, making my energy crash not long after dinner. Oskar bundled me up and carried me back to his bed, which was easily the most comfortable one I'd ever slept in. He still had work to do, so he made sure I was okay before leaving.

I slept so deeply that I didn't feel him come into bed with me at some point in the night, spooning behind me. His warm, bare chest enveloped my back, warming me to perfection. Waking up in bed with him before had been great, but waking up with him as my mate was truly perfect.

"Morning," I said, rolling over and burying my face in his chest.

"Morning. Sleep well?" He kissed my forehead.

"Very well." I yawned. "What time is it anyway?"

"It's nine. You've been out for more than twelve hours." He rubbed my back.

"Seriously?" I sat up on one elbow. The tank top I wore to bed was twisted around my middle, the neckline dipped low to the point where one of my breasts was nearly popping out. Oskar's eyes lingered there, a slow smile coming across his face.

My cheeks flushed when I felt his arousal, both against my stomach and through our mate bond.

"Strange, isn't it?" he said. "The emotional bond."

"Strange, but amazing." I kissed him, throwing one leg over his hip. "I like knowing when you're full of shit."

"You already did a good job of sensing that." He laughed, the sound of it making me smile.

"True." I slid a hand between us toward the bulge in his boxer-briefs, but he stopped me.

"I'd love to, but we've made some plans for today," he said. "We're having a meeting with the Alphas of the rabbit and falcon shifters. I've put in a temporary rabbit shifter Ruler since Anja is in custody, so they'll join, too. And Gunnar is out of his coma, but we're not sure if he'll be completely up to attending."

"That's great!" I missed Gunnar in a weird way. Being able to see him up and lively again was going to feel amazing.

"And I called Filip," Oskar added. "He'll be here later this afternoon."

I nearly choked on my own saliva. "Filip is coming here? Of his own accord?"

"Yes, with Mylee and their daughter." He tucked my hair behind my ear. It was getting too long. "I figured we'd have to talk about this sooner or later, so we might as well get it done now. I want you to move here with me as soon as you can."

"Of course." I paused. "I'll have to get a lot of sweaters."

"It's not too bad in the winter. We can keep each other warm." He kissed me again, making my heart expand. "But we should get ready. Freya will brief you before the meeting."

"Okay."

I slid out of bed, stretching, and went to the bathroom. Oskar's shower was enormous, more than big enough for someone of his size. He came in behind me, naked, and helped me with the faucets. The water poured down on our heads, hot and steamy.

"Are we showering together to be efficient, or did you just want to see me naked?" I asked, admiring the way the water slid down his muscular chest.

"Both?" He grabbed a bottle of body wash and a cloth. "Though I almost regret it, because we don't have time to fool around."

"We don't have a *lot* of time, but I'd say we have enough." I sat down on the bench in the corner, motioning for him to come toward me.

He grinned, stepping close to me and resting his hands on the wall above my head. His cock was at just the right height for me to take him into my mouth. The sound of him sucking in a breath and biting back a groan spurred me to take him even deeper. I worked him with my hand as well, making him gasp and pump his hips forward as if his body had taken over his mind. He stopped himself from fucking my mouth to the point where I choked, though I could have taken him that way.

The rush of excitement and arousal flowing between the two of us soaked me between my thighs to the point where I had to reach between them and touch myself. I loved knowing just how much I was pleasuring him, as if I were in his body and he were in mine.

He abruptly pulled his cock from my mouth and picked me up, holding me in mid-air as he slid into me. The sudden change made the thrill of him inside me again even better. I held onto him as he slid me up and down his cock, his hands under my ass. The rough momentum he built up made me gasp with each thrust. I couldn't catch my breath, especially when he shifted me to one arm and rubbed my clit with his free hand.

I cried out so loudly that it echoed across the bathroom, my head tilting back and bumping the wall. It didn't break the pleasure, though. It was perfect.

"Come for me, Daria," he said, his voice rough and his breathing labored. "Come on my cock."

His words took me over the edge, the climax more intense than anything I'd ever felt. He braced me against the wall and pounded into me so hard that my back squeaked against the tile. My orgasm faded, then crested again as he came as well.

Both of us slumped against the wall, trying to catch our breath. Eventually, he started laughing, which made me start to laugh, too, even though I had no idea what was funny.

"It's just that I never thought anything could feel that good. And that perfect," he said, helping me to my feet. "And the fact that you're my mate is still surreal. We're going to have more of that forever."

"I know." I went on my tiptoes and gave him a peck on the lips. "But right now, we have some meetings to attend, so we should actually hurry."

We finished showering and dressing—someone had brought all of my clothes into his room at some point—then went to the largest meeting room in the palace. Freya, a guard, an attendant, and a male I didn't recognize were the only ones inside. The male was enormous, so I assumed he was a wolf, a dragon, or another species of predator.

"Good morning," Freya said. "I hope you rested well."

"I did." I glanced at the male who I didn't know.

"This is my husband, Mikhail," Freya said, putting her hand on his shoulder. "He owns a tea and coffee business, so he's supplying some special blends for today."

"Oh!" I blinked. "I never knew you were married."

"We've been together for centuries, so we don't bother with rings," Mikhail said, extending his huge hand to me. "Nice to meet you."

"Nice to meet you as well." My face heated up, then heated up more when I remembered that Oskar felt my embarrassment. I'd have to explain myself later. The sibling-type love he felt towards her obliterated the last of my worries that they'd ever been involved.

"I'll leave you to it," Mikhail said, leaning in and kissing Freya on the lips. "Good luck."

"Thanks. Good to see you," Oskar said. Mikhail bowed his head and left.

"Sit," Freya said, gesturing toward the seat adjacent to Oskar's at the head of the table. "Let me get you some tea, since we have a lot to cover."

The attendant poured me some tea, which was the best I'd ever had, while Freya went over the parameters for the meeting. All we had to do was make sure the rabbits and the falcons were going to move forward with peace at the forefront, not their longstanding rivalries.

The door opened in the middle of our conversation. I started to tell whoever it was that we were busy, but it was Gunnar in a wheelchair, being pushed by a healer. He still looked rough, his frame frail and his eyes bloodshot, but he was up, showered, and dressed. And he was smiling.

"Gunnar, how are you feeling?" I asked, standing up.

"Like hot garbage, but it's better than being in a coma." He snorted. "A lot's happened, yeah?"

We filled him in on everything, and he listened the way he had in the days after his talk with Oskar, the one that had changed his perspective. The poison was to blame for his sudden regression, thankfully. He was all in again.

"You're sure you want to be in the meeting?" I asked Gunnar. "You just got out of a coma, so I doubt anyone would blame you for skipping out."

"I'm sure. I want to listen, at least. And show everyone I care." He swallowed. He'd lost a few pounds, so the bobbing of his Adam's apple was more prominent. "Because I really do care."

"I can tell." I wanted to hug him, but I held myself back. "High Ruler Oskar and I will take the lead, though. Just jump in whenever."

Gunnar nodded, his expression serious but determined. I was proud of him just for throwing himself into it. He wasn't perfect, but he was trying.

The falcon shifter Alphas and rabbit shifter Alphas came in, sitting on separate sides of the table. My stomach twisted in knots. The rabbit shifter Alphas—at least the ones who hadn't been involved in the plan to destabilize the falcon shifters—were more likely to lean toward peace, but I wasn't sure about the falcons. They'd been so difficult, in part because of the discord the rabbit shifters had created. But they weren't the most cooperative bunch.

"Thank you for coming on such short notice," Oskar said,

standing at the head of the table. "In light of everything that's happened between the rabbit shifters and falcon shifters recently, I'd like to propose a formal truce between the two groups."

"We agree," the temporary rabbit shifter Ruler said. "We'd also like to formally apologize for Ruler Anja's actions. We'd like to cooperate more in the future to avoid bloodshed and non-violent conflict."

"I agree, too," Gunnar said. His voice was rough from not being used, but he spoke loudly enough to be heard. "I'd like my reign to be a peaceful one. We don't have to resort to violence or push each other into unnecessary conflict when we can just talk to each other."

Pasha, the least problematic falcon shifter Alpha, agreed as well. The others were quieter, but once Ulla and, to my surprise, Artem, fell into line, Klaus and Annelli did, too, though reluctantly.

We spent the next few hours detailing the terms of the truce. Aside from a few tempers flaring from the falcons over certain terms, they came to a mutual agreement. Gunnar did well, though he had a long way to go to gain the full trust of the Alphas.

The meeting ended with a light lunch, plus more tea that Mikhail had brought from his travels. I sat next to Oskar the entire time, enjoying even a moment like this with him. The more we were together, the more I appreciated the little things about how he ruled. He was enormously powerful, but he was able to bridge that gap if he wanted to.

"I'm not sure if it was the long meeting or the residual serum or the fact that Filip and Mylee will be here in an hour or two, but I'm exhausted again," I said once we were back in Oskar's office for a break. I flopped down onto the couch in the corner, and he joined me, putting his arm around my shoulders.

"I'm preemptively exhausted and annoyed about their visit," he said. "But I'm going to try for us."

"I know you will." I buried my head against the side of his neck, smiling. "Before I came here, I told Filip I was preemptively annoyed. Pre-annoyed."

He laughed, the sound warm and comforting "Really? I don't

blame you. I was nervous and annoyed, too, even though I was the one who requested that you come to Iceland."

"What are you planning to say to Fillip? How did he react to us being mates?" I asked, smoothing my hand over his cashmere sweater.

"I didn't mention that we were mates yet. I just said I needed to meet with him."

"Oh, gods, Oskar."

"I know." He let his head fall back against the couch. "But I doubt he would have come if I'd told him over the phone. He wouldn't have believed me, and you were asleep."

"He's in for a shock."

A smirk spread across Oskar's face. "It'll be satisfying to watch. And you can't even be mad at me about it, because it's a positive surprise."

I pinched his side, just hard enough to tickle. "You promised you'd be good."

"I know, I know. I will be." He kissed my forehead.

We decompressed in silence, stealing kisses from time to time, until Oskar's guard came to take us to the room where Filip and Mylee were waiting. We held hands the whole walk over, both of us buzzing with anxiety. I missed Filip and Mylee and was looking forward to seeing them, but how were they going to react?

One of Filip's guards, a warlock named Hans, was posted outside. He smiled when he saw me, then his eyes widened when he noticed our mate bond.

"Hi, Hans," I said." It's good to see you."

"It's good to see you, too." He hesitated with his hand on the doorknob.

I nodded for him to go on.

He opened the door to reveal Filip and Mylee. Audra must have been with a nanny. Filip smiled, but it quickly fell to confusion, then mild horror when he realized that Oskar and I were holding hands *and* we were mates.

"Congratulations!" Mylee said, coming over to hug me. She still smelled like the beach, even after being on a plane for hours.

"This isn't a joke," Filip said, his green eyes wide. "Is this why you called me here? Because you're...mates?"

"Yes," Oskar said, guiding me over to the small couch across from where Mylee and Filip were sitting.

Mylee was beaming, as I expected her to, but Filip's reaction made me nervous. Mate bonds just happened—we didn't choose who they were with. Being mad at me about it was stupid. But I was getting ahead of myself.

"I'd like to propose a truce of sorts," Oskar said, his words stilted. "Because Daria means everything to me, and you're her closest friend and High Ruler. We have to put our past behind us."

Filip considered Oskar's words, looking between the two of us. Oskar's nerves simmered underneath his calm exterior.

"I agree," Filip said, as if the words hurt him. "For Daria's sake."

"Exactly." Oskar squeezed my hand. "And I'd like her to move here with me. You understand how painful it is to be apart from your mate."

Filip rested his hand on Mylee's leg. "I do. But I also know that I need my second-in-command. I've been dealing with a temporary aide, but he isn't at Daria's level."

"I can go back for a while to train my replacement," I said. "Will that help?"

"It will." Filip's expression finally softened. He'd been much less abrasive since he'd been with Mylee, so seeing this look on his face still affected me. "But that won't change the fact that we'll miss you."

"I know. I'll miss you all, too, but I'll definitely visit," I said.

Filip sized Oskar up. "You'll be good to her, yes?"

"Of course. She's my mate." Oskar's voice had an edge to it, so I squeezed his hand to get him to calm down. "We'll do just fine."

"Good." Filip took in a deep breath and let it out. "I can't believe this. Oskar, of all males."

"I would have been shocked, too, if you'd told me before I came here." I smiled. "But it's undeniable."

"I know," Filip said. "I'm happy you're happy, Daria."

A tiny tinge of surprise, then pleasure, flowed from Oskar's side of our mate bond. I suppressed a smile. Maybe they'd get along eventually, but for now, I was just glad we'd found a middle ground.

EPILOGUE
OSKAR

Two Years Later

"Here, take this," I said, winding another scarf around Daria's neck.

"Thanks." She pulled it up around her face. "How is it this cold? It's supposed to be warming up by now."

"Because not everywhere has lava-like air like Florida." I tucked the scarf around her neck more. "Come on, let's keep walking."

She looped her arm in mine as we hiked up a hill to a spot with an incredible view, where I had a surprise waiting for her. I'd had a getaway cabin built for us for whenever being in the palace got tiring. She loved the views in Iceland, even if she hated the cold, and this area had some of the best on the entire island. Getting up there in our shifted forms was easier, but I liked being able to hold onto her like this instead of having her flying above me.

In the year since our mate bond had snapped into place, she'd slowly but surely gotten used to living in Iceland. Once she'd had the chance to explore the island, taking in all of its natural beauty, she came to love it as much as I did. We'd spent hours sitting outside, bundled up under a blanket, watching the northern lights or looking up at the stars. Plus, she'd finally expanded her wardrobe enough that dressing in layers wasn't a problem at all.

"You're not going to tell me what this is?" she asked.

"That would ruin the surprise. Just another five minutes."

We trudged up the hill. I was glad that I'd decided to build our cabin here instead of on a flat plain. Her vision was so sharp that she would have seen what I was doing from here.

"Close your eyes," I said as we approached the final hill.

"Okay, they're closed."

"Hold onto me and pick your feet up." I slowly guided her up the hill. Once we were in view, I stopped us. "Open your eyes."

Daria did and gasped, delight brightening her brown eyes. "Is this for us?"

"It is. A little getaway spot." I pulled her along. "Our staff has already brought our things, so we have everything we need. I've been planning this surprise for a while."

"I'm completely surprised." She beamed. "Show me around."

I pressed my hand to the door to activate the protection charm on it. The cabin looked much bigger on the inside than it appeared to be, all light woods and bright colors. I'd had the back wall made up of windows to give the fullest view off the hill.

"It's stunning, Oskar," she said, going to the windows. She put her hand to them, her mouth slightly open in awe. "I love it. So much. And it's so warm!"

I laughed. "We have a fireplace, too."

"I've always wanted one of these!" She ran her hand along the mantle. "I can't wait to relax here. What made you decide to build this now?"

"We need a place for a quick escape when we need to get away from our responsibilities," I said, taking her hand and guiding her down to the couch that faced the view. "So, I found this spot and had the house built."

Ever since we had helped make the truce between the rabbits and the falcons, we'd had a number of extra tasks to put the truce into action. Gunnar had fully recovered and had finished his training with

Daria after she had gone home and trained her replacement with Filip. And Gunnar still needed some help, so Daria supported him from time to time.

We'd also put Ruler Anja to death for plotting against Ruler Gunnar. It was painful for me, but she'd gone too far. The other rabbit shifters, witches, and warlocks involved were given much lighter sentences, especially Astrid. She no longer had any security clearances at my headquarters, but her willingness to confess had helped us wrap up the case quickly.

The falcon shifter Alphas had mostly stuck to their agreement to be peaceful, though Daria also helped me keep an eye on them in that regard. All of the Alphas understood how closely they were being watched and kept themselves in line.

Daria had taken on so much so quickly that she sometimes got burnt out—hence the cabin. She already looked right at home.

"Let's look at the rest of it," she said, getting to her feet. "Is there enough room for guests? Maybe we could have Freya and Mikhail come stay sometime."

"Yeah, we could."

Since Daria was my mate and was highly skilled, Freya had stepped down as my second-in-command, so she and Mikhail had more time to run his tea business. She would always be a part of my inner circle, giving guidance when necessary, but now she had the freedom to travel. I missed her quiet presence and her ability to make tough calls, but knowing she and Mikhail were happy helped.

Daria peeked into the rooms lining the hallway—the master bedroom, the bathroom, another small living room, and finally, a second guest room.

"Oh, there are two!" Daria turned, her grin wicked. "Maybe Filip and Mylee could stay with us, too."

"Maybe." The thought pained me, but not as much as it would have before.

We'd gone back to Florida for more than a dozen times in the past two years, so I had gotten a full dose of Filip. Some days, I'd wanted to fling myself into the ocean to get away from him, and vice versa, probably.

I still didn't like him that much, though Mylee was surprisingly delightful. Then again, if Filip's mate were too similar to him, the entire southern half of the United States would have sunk into the ocean from the weight of their egos.

But I put up with him for Daria. And fine, he was funny every once in a while. Also, the way he ruled was admirable, not that I'd ever tell him.

Daria turned around at the end of the hallway and pushed me backward, a playful smirk on her face. That face only meant good things, even if she looked mischievous. She guided me into our master bedroom, which was on the side of the house. Its view was equally as stunning as the one out back.

I sat down on the bed, pulling her on top of me before she pushed me onto the bed. She squeaked in surprise and straddled me, her entire being alight with happiness. Seeing her like this gave my life an even deeper purpose than before. She was my greatest ally and understood me like no one else ever had. We were one soul in two bodies.

"Thank you," she whispered, kissing me on the forehead, then the lips. "It's perfect."

I smiled. "Anything for you."

～

What to Read Next:
Veiled Realm: Complete Series Romance Collection
The rulers of the Veiled Realm are powerful, drop-dead gorgeous,
and lethal if you threaten their mates.

OTHER BOOKS YOU WILL LOVE

Veiled Realm: Complete Series Romance Collection
The rulers of the Veiled Realm are powerful, drop-dead gorgeous,
and lethal if you threaten their mates.

Fated Shifters: Romance Collection
True Mates. Secret Babies. Fake Relationships.
A shifter collection full of skin-tingling romances that are sexy,
suspenseful, and action-packed!

**Love, Lies and Billionaires: Complete Contemporary Romance
Collection**
Smoking Hot. Damaged. Forbidden.
Take a wild, toe-curling ride with these eight, full-length novels...

SECRET WOODS BOOKS

Receive a FREE paranormal romance eBook by visiting our website and signing up for our mailing list:

SecretWoodsBooks.com

By signing up for our mailing list, you'll receive a FREE paranormal romance eBook. The newsletter will also provide information on upcoming books and special offers.